My name is Barry Allen, and I am the fastest man alive. A freak accident sent a lightning bolt into my lab one night, dousing me with electricity and chemicals, gifting me with superspeed. Since then, I've used my powers to fight the good fight, protecting my city, my world, and my universe from all manner of threats. I've stared down crazed speedsters, time-traveling techno-magicians, and every sort of thief, crook, and lunatic you can imagine.

With the help of my friends and my adopted family, I run S.T.A.R. Labs, a hub of super-science, and use it as a staging base to keep Central City safe from those who would cause it harm.

I've traveled to not one but two different futures, and I've seen the amazing heights to which humanity will soar. In the present, I do everything I can to help get us there.

I am . . .

THE FLASH

BY BARRY LYGA

1SH™

CROSSOVER CRISIS

GREEN ARROW'S PERFECT SHOT

AMULET BOOKS
NEW YORK

The Library of Congress has cataloged the hardcover edition as follows:

Names: Lyga, Barry, author.
Title: Green Arrow's perfect shot / by Barry Lyga.
Description: New York, NY : Amulet Books, [2019] | Series: The Flash: crossover crisis ; book 1 | Summary: "When the Green Arrow needs help tracking down a sinister bomber in Star City, speedster Barry Allen is out the door in a flash. But as the Flash saves the day with his friends on Team Arrow, a huge dimensional rift appears over his hometown of Central City—and thousands of refugees with superspeed come pouring out. Can the combined skills of Team Arrow and the Flash's friends at S.T.A.R. Labs manage the chaos long enough to stop the rift from tearing their universe apart?" —Provided by publisher. Identifiers: LCCN 2019011702 | ISBN 9781419737381 (hardback) Subjects: | CYAC: Superheroes—Fiction. | Adventure and adventurers—Fiction. | BISAC: JUVENILE FICTION / Action & Adventure / General. | JUVENILE FICTION / Comics & Graphic Novels / Media Tie-In. Classification: LCC PZ7.L97967 Gre 2019 | DDC [Fic]—dc23

Paperback ISBN 978-1-4197-4694-9

Cover illustraton by César Moreno
Book design by John Passineau

Published in paperback in 2021 by Amulet Books, an imprint of ABRAMS. Originally published in hardcover by Amulet Books in 2019. All rights reserved. No portion of this book may be reproduced, stored in a retrieval system, or transmitted in any form or by any means, mechanical, electronic, photocopying, recording, or otherwise, without written permission from the publisher.

Printed and bound in U.S.A.
10 9 8 7 6 5 4 3 2 1

Amulet Books are available at special discounts when purchased in quantity for premiums and promotions as well as fundraising or educational use. Special editions can also be created to specification. For details, contact specialsales@abramsbooks.com or the address below.

Amulet Books® is a registered trademark of Harry N. Abrams, Inc.

ABRAMS The Art of Books
195 Broadway, New York, NY 10007
abramsbooks.com

TEAM FLASH

THE FLASH (BARRY ALLEN)
IRIS WEST-ALLEN
VIBE (CISCO RAMON)
DR. CAITLIN SNOW
DETECTIVE JOE WEST

TEAM ARROW

GREEN ARROW (OLIVER QUEEN)
SPARTAN (JOHN DIGGLE)
MR. TERRIFIC (CURTIS HOLT)
OVERWATCH (FELICITY SMOAK)
WILD DOG (RENE RAMIREZ)
BLACK CANARY (DINAH DRAKE)

THE LEGENDS
OF TOMORROW

WHITE CANARY (SARA LANCE)
THE ATOM (RAY PALMER)
HEAT WAVE (MICK RORY)

AND

MADAME XANADU

SARA LANCE, THE WHITE CANARY, blinked in surprise as Ray Palmer burst onto the bridge of the *Waverider*, waving his hands excitedly. "Wake up!" he yelled. "Wake up!"

"The Legends," a ragtag group of time travelers charged with monitoring and protecting Time itself, weren't currently on a mission. Sara was in charge of the team—as "in charge" as she could be, considering the Legends' resistance to order—but this was downtime, so she was lounging, having swapped out her white leather combat togs for a more comfortable and loose-fitting set of "relaxation wear" from the year 2190. Her dirty-blonde hair spilled over her shoulders, and those same shoulders were actually loose for once, not taut and tense.

Now her shoulders bunched a tiny bit at Ray's intrusion into her peace and quiet.

"I wasn't asleep," Sara said irritably, gesturing for Ray to calm down. She hadn't been sleeping in the captain's chair, but she *had* been so deep in thought that Ray had managed to enter the bridge before she could react. Not good. He was a friend, not a foe, but she prided herself on her constant awareness, her inability to be ambushed. The training that she'd endured at the hands of the League of Assassins had left scars both physical and emotional, but one of the benefits to the tutelage of a secret society of ninjas was that you were rarely sneaked up on.

"Wake up anyway!" Ray cried. Off-mission, he wore stonewashed jeans and a T-shirt from the Rolling Stones' *Steel Wheels* tour kickoff at Toad's Place in 1989. "Gideon! Show her that stuff we were just looking at."

"Of course, Mr. Palmer." Gideon, the *Waverider*'s built-in artificial intelligence, conjured a series of holographic images. They floated around the central interface node on the bridge.

"This is huge!" Ray gesticulated wildly at the images. Tall and classically handsome, with a boyish mien and too-perfect hair, Ray exuded youthful enthusiasm to the point of hyperbolic excitement, but there was usually a basis for it.

Sara leaned forward, frowning as she scrutinized the

images. She couldn't quite make out what had Ray so riled up at the moment.

"They were right!" Ray crowed. "Barry Allen and Cisco Ramon were right!"

Sara clucked her tongue. "Did you think they were *lying* to us?"

Ray calmed down long enough to pull a wounded face. "Of course not! But they could have been mistaken."

With a sigh, Sara hauled herself out of the captain's chair and paced around the holograms. Time for business, she supposed. For an employee of the government's top secret Time Bureau, there was no such thing as "off the clock." Which, she knew, was a pretty bad pun for a time traveler, but it was still true.

"So, these images . . ." she prompted Ray.

". . . are representations of the data Gideon and I have been compiling," Ray responded. "According to Barry and Cisco, the universe we live in has a duplicate, a near-identical twin. Not a parallel universe like the ones we're familiar with, but rather an entire alternate timeline. In *that* timeline, the Flash went back in time and saved his mother from being killed by the Reverse-Flash, and the temporal consequences were so great that it created something called Flashpoint."

"Gideon!" Sara called. "Reference Flashpoint, please."

A translucent, almost featureless face materialized from

thin air, the visual interface to Gideon. "I'm sorry, Captain Lance," Gideon said soothingly. "There is no reference data in the Time Masters' or Time Bureau's databases for Flashpoint."

"This is what I'm saying!" Ray said, walking through Gideon's hologram. "In *our* timeline, there never was a Flashpoint." He flung a hand out at the images he and Gideon had projected. "According to all this data, though, this alternate timeline actually exists. And when the Barry Allen of that other timeline tried to fix his Flashpoint mistake, there was a knock-on effect—the universe didn't return to its original state. It's like nothing we've seen before. And there's no record of anything like it having *ever* happened. When the Legion of Doom created an alternate reality, we were able to set the universe back to rights. But this . . . It's almost as though the entire universe experienced a timequake from inside the temporal zone. It's a singular event, unique across the Multiverse!"

Ray was breathing hard as he finished, and Sara could scarcely blame him. As time travelers, she and her team had traversed the length and breadth of the universe, tinkering with Time itself. Occasionally they'd glitched up the time stream, but they'd always been able to fix it. Now there was another whole timeline out there that someone had tried to fix . . . and couldn't.

"What do we do about it?" she mused, staring at the data. An entire timeline . . . "Do we go back and try to prevent Allen from saving his mother in the first place? Restore the flow of time?"

"That's what *he* tried," Ray protested. "It didn't work. Besides, I don't even know how we would get into that other timeline in the first place. The *Waverider* is attuned to our timeline and designed to cruise *this* time stream. It would be like . . ." He drifted off as he cast about for a metaphor.

"It would be like being in a boat on one river and trying to hop it over land to another river," Sara supplied.

Ray shrugged. "I guess that works. Or doesn't, as the case may be."

She wished Kid Flash—Wally West—were still with them. Like Barry Allen, Wally was a speedster, and he had a speedster's unique perspective on time travel. He was also the Flash's adopted brother and had spent a lot of time with the gang at S.T.A.R. Labs, where the Flash and his crew did all kinds of superhero science. Kid Flash's input could be useful. He'd become part of her team a little while back but right now was on some well-deserved R&R in the 1960s.

And yeah, Sara, like the League of Assassins would have let you take a vacation when trouble was brewing.

Gnawing at her bottom lip, she considered her options. Was this alternate timeline a threat to their own? Usually, her crew made a point of erasing such mistakes, but there had been occasions where they'd been forced to *create* time instabilities rather than destroy them. Maybe this alternate timeline was a natural part of the order of the vast, unknowable universe. Or universe*s*.

And maybe these kinds of metaphysical questions were a little much for a simple party girl from what had once been called Starling City.

"I'm canceling Kid Flash's shore leave," she decided. "Gideon, lay in a course for—"

The *Waverider* suddenly juddered, as though it were a sailing vessel that had run aground on a reef. Sara grabbed a handhold and, with her other hand, snagged Ray's wrist to keep him from stumbling away and falling down.

"What was that?" Ray demanded.

"Gideon!" Sara commanded. "Sitrep!"

The ship was still shaking. Sara swung Ray into one of the bridge's seats, then hauled herself back to the captain's chair and buckled in. "Gideon! I said *sitrep!*"

"Situation report," Gideon began as the *Waverider* continued its quaking. "We appear to have collided with a time bolus."

"Now I've heard everything," Sara muttered. She slapped some controls on the arm of her chair. "Route around it."

"We appear to be caught *within* it, Captain Lance."

Groaning, Sara adjusted some more controls. Gideon was an excellent pilot and a terrific resource, but at the end of the day, it couldn't think creatively. The ship needed a human at the helm to truly exploit its potential.

"Ray!" she called. "Thoughts?"

From his chair, Ray scanned the available data. "It's like concentrated temporal energy," he said, his teeth clacking as the ship vibrated madly. "It'll shake us to pieces."

Just then, the door to the bridge opened. Mick Rory stood there, one hand clutching a handhold, the other clinging to a grease-dripping ham, egg, and cheese sandwich. His normally sour expression was even more sour than usual. A dollop of melted cheese had wound up on his bald head and was oozing down over one ear. As Heat Wave, he'd started out as a villain. Then he worked with the Legends until he made it about halfway to hero. Gruff and blunt, he could always be counted on to . . . well, to be gruff and blunt.

"Did we hit another dinosaur?" he demanded. "Because I'm not gonna be the one to hose the reptile guts off the windshield this time."

Windshield . . . Sara snapped her head up from the data displays and looked through the large, reinforced windows at the nose of the *Waverider*. They resembled glass but were actually an exotic, transparent futuristic form of a metal called inertron. Toughest stuff in the universe, or so she'd been told.

The data screens were changing too rapidly to be any help. But through the window, she beheld a flashing, flickering kaleidoscope, a whirl and smear of colors whipping all around the hull. "What *is* this?" she asked no one in particular.

"Chronal bleed!" Ray called out from his station.

"So, it's a no on the dinosaur?" Mick asked. It took him three tries, what with the ship's constant shaking, but he managed to get the sandwich into his mouth and take a bite.

"There's some kind of pulse of temporal energy moving at trans-tachyon velocities. It's moving so fast . . ." Ray paused. "It has so much momentum, it must have come from extremely far in the future. And this 'time bolus' is an artifact of its travel."

"So what do we do about it?"

Even as she asked, though, the ship suddenly broke free. Sara checked her readouts. Something was wrong. They should have drifted loose once free of the bolus, but according to her instruments, they were moving into the future. *Very* quickly.

Once the ship stopped shaking, Mick sighed in relief. "OK, then. Back to watching the 1986 World Series. I love it when that ball goes right through Buckner's legs." He left the bridge and the door shut behind him.

"That was close," Ray said. "We—"

"Ray!" Sara projected her readout onto the main screen. "Look at this. We're not clear yet."

"What's going on, Gideon?" Ray asked.

"Mr. Palmer, we appear to be caught up in a chronal inversion. The energy projection from the future is so powerful that the universe's need for equilibrium has created an equally potent stream going in the opposite direction. And the *Waverider* is caught in it."

"Out of the frying pan . . ." Sara muttered. "See if you can engage the retro-thrusters and slow us down—"

"Collision imminent!" Gideon warned. "Collision imminent!"

"*Now* a dinosaur?" Ray asked, bewildered. "Or a— Holy . . . Sara! Look!"

Sara pulled her attention away from the controls and stared through the windshield. "Oh my God . . ." she whispered. "What is *that*?"

"It appears to be some sort of shield or wall," Gideon supplied smoothly. "A barrier of some sort athwart the time stream itself."

"How is that even possible?" Sara asked. She was trying to engage retro-thrusters, side-thrusters, but nothing could budge them from their course.

"It looks like a . . . *curtain* . . ." Ray started.

"Three seconds to impact," Gideon informed them.

"A *curtain* . . ." he said again. Sara felt beads of sweat on her forehead as she stabbed over and over at the thruster controls, as though punching them harder would make them work.

"Two . . ." said Gideon. "One . . ."

1

STAR CITY IS IN TROUBLE."

Oliver Queen snorted and glanced over his shoulder. Down in the bowels of the Bunker, concealed beneath the Palmer Technologies building, he was alone with only Felicity Smoak, his partner in both life and in crime-fighting. They'd been married more than a year now, having exchanged their vows after an invasion of superpowered beings from an Earth that had been conquered by Nazis.

It felt ridiculous even to think such a thing, but it was true—it had happened. And it was also true—and obvious—that Star City was in trouble.

"Tell me something I don't know," he said with gentle sarcasm.

At her workstation, Felicity clucked her tongue. "Be nice, and I'll show you something you've never seen before."

Oliver arched an eyebrow.

Felicity blushed. "Oh, wow. *That* came out wrong! Anyway . . ." She pounded at her keyboard for a moment. "There. How do you like *them* arrows, Green Apple? I mean . . ."

Oliver turned his attention to the gigantic computer monitor he stood before. It displayed a satellite image of the part of Star City closest to what had been called the Glades. A few years back, Malcolm Merlyn had destroyed that area of the city, and the entire region was still recovering. On the edge of Star City, abutting the wreck and the chasm that had once been the Glades, was a series of rapidly abandoned apartment complexes. As leases ran out, tenants were fleeing as quickly as moving vans could move them. No one wanted to live in proximity to the spot where the city had imploded.

But the current problem, the current trouble, wasn't just a question of urban flight or a declining tax base. When *those* sorts of problems came up, Oliver deferred to the city government. He'd been mayor once—it hadn't lasted—and he had some measure of respect for the people who did the hard work of running this city.

Sometimes, though . . .

Sometimes, life required a more direct approach.

"Here's an overlay for ya . . ." Felicity tapped a few more

keys. Oliver nodded his thanks and studied the screen.

There were three gaps in the satellite map, open pits in the cityscape, like the empty spaces where teeth had been pulled. Felicity's overlay put circles in those spots, along with data readouts. One week ago, there'd been buildings in those spots.

No more. Someone had blown them up over the past week, knocking them down with ruthless efficiency. Fortunately, they had all been empty at the time. No loss of life.

Yet.

"And here . . ." Felicity said, typing.

The overlay changed. Now four more circles appeared, this time over buildings that were still standing.

"Using the forensic information pulled from the three crime scenes," Felicity said, "and then comparing building records from the municipal database, I project that the bomber's next target will be one of these four buildings. All of them were built around the same time, and all of them have the same structural defects that made the first three so easy for him to knock down."

Oliver sighed. Four possible targets. "I can't let this guy rack up another win," he said. "That neighborhood's been through enough already, and the city has never really done right by it. We need to stop this serial bomber before he does it again. We've been lucky that no one's been hurt yet, but our luck can't hold out forever."

Felicity joined him at the screen and looped her arm through his. His entire body was taut, rigid. The darkness within Oliver propelled him to great deeds and good works . . . but it was still a darkness. Felicity had come to terms with it, but sometimes—as now—the very physical manifestation of his anger and intensity could be eye-opening.

"We'll figure it out," she promised.

He shook his head. "No time to figure it out. If he sticks to his pattern, he'll take down another building tonight. We need to get the whole team together, set watches for all four of those . . ." He drifted off.

"What?" she asked.

"No good. If we don't want to scare him off, we'll need to watch from afar. Nearby rooftops, maybe. But by the time we identify him and the target, he could trigger the explosives. We wouldn't get there fast enough."

Felicity laughed and pulled away from him, digging into her pocket. "Did you say *fast enough*?"

"What do you . . . Oh." Oliver's eyes widened when he saw what she produced from her pocket—her phone.

"You know someone who's plenty fast, right?" She waggled the phone in the air between them, grinning.

Oliver surrendered without much of a fight. She was right, after all. "OK, fine. I'll call the Flash."

2

MEANWHILE, HUNDREDS OF MILES away in Central City, it was lunchtime and there was a superhero battle going on at the intersection of Kanigher Avenue and Baron Street. A crowd had gathered to watch, snapping selfies, shooting videos, and streaming the whole thing live to those places in the world that were so much more boring.

Barry Allen—the Flash—spared a hundredth of a second to turn his face to one guy's cell phone and flash a V-for-Victory sign. It happened so fast that no one would ever notice it, unless the guy was shooting at 120 frames per second and someday decided to slow down the video and go through it frame by frame. If he did, he'd have a little surprise waiting for him. It would probably still be blurry by dint of Barry's velocity, but hey—superspeed meant that you could do stuff like that. Even in the middle of a fight.

Barry dashed away from his unknowing videographer and dodged a laser blast. The pavement where he had been standing briefly liquefied, splashed up into the air, then solidified again, blooming like a black, tarry flower in the middle of the street. He made a mental note to fix that when this fight was over. No sense letting traffic get snarled at this intersection, right?

He was battling a guy named Roy Bivolo, who called himself Rainbow Raider. Originally, Bivolo had developed a metahuman ability to fill people with rage just by looking at them. Now his emotion-manipulating power had expanded, allowing him to induce a whole range of feelings.

Worse than that, he'd managed to gull seven other people into joining him on his perpetual quest for ill-gotten riches. The "Seven Deadly Tints" each wore a costume with a different color of the rainbow and carried—get this— color-coordinated laser cannons to back up their boss's thieving. Right now, Bivolo was sneaking into an art gallery while Barry was keeping the Tints from hurting anyone out on the streets. He'd already taken down Red, Yellow, and Blue. Violet, Indigo, Green, and Orange were still at large.

Barry pushed a young woman out of the path of one of Orange's laser blasts. It was sort of ego-affirming to have eager throngs of citizens watch him take on the latest super-villain threat, but adding innocent bystanders to a combat zone was less than ideal. As best he could tell, there were something like a hundred people gathered around: each one of them supremely confident in the Flash's ability to save the day and keep them safe, each one of them in danger.

He did the math in his head. A hundred people . . . Figure it would take maybe half a second each to get them out of the danger zone . . . He could do it faster, but there was always the fear of whiplash when moving people that fast. And you never knew who in the crowd had some kind of genetic heart defect or an undiagnosed brain aneurysm that could pop from the shock of a superspeed jostle.

So instead of moving the innocents, he went for the Tints. He raced to Orange's side, grabbed her by the elbow, and ran a block up Kanigher Avenue in less time than it took to blink. By the time Orange realized what he'd done, she was already bound to a lamppost with a length of sturdy rope Barry had grabbed from a nearby hardware store.

"Hey!" she yelled. "I think you dislocated my shoulder! You can't just—!"

Barry touched her head briefly and vibrated just enough to bounce her brain against the inside of her skull. She passed out, and he was back to the scene of the fight in an instant.

Violet, Indigo, and Green had turned their backs to one

another and held their laser cannons at the ready, eager to pull the trigger at the sight of the slightest sign of a red-and-yellow blur or a crackle of electricity.

Scanning the area, Barry noticed a sewer cover. He wrinkled his nose. It had been more than a year, but he still remembered—in far too much detail—descending into the stench of the Central City sewer system in order to capture Dr. Herbert Hynde, the serial killer known as Earthworm. He wasn't eager to relive the experience.

Well, no one ever said being a superhero would be neat and tidy.

He vibrated through the manhole cover in the street, turning solid just long enough to land on the access ladder, then leaped up and at an angle, vibrating again to pass through the street from underneath.

His guesstimate of angles and distances had been spot-on; he emerged from beneath the pavement of Kanigher Avenue in the center of the Tints' circle, then spun like a top at superspeed, fists extended. *Clonk! Clonk! Clonk!* In the space of two seconds, he'd smacked each of them ten times.

The three remaining Tints crumpled to the ground like pinwheels in a too-strong wind.

The crowd exploded into applause. Barry hammed it up, offering a short bow. But he knew he wasn't done yet.

• • •

Mega! was Central City's newest and most talked-about art gallery, with a hip pop art sign that resembled an old-fashioned comic book word balloon, the word MEGA! exploding from its confines, as though too awesome to be contained.

During the workweek, the gallery didn't open until five. Right now, though, the door was kicked in. Rainbow Raider was many things, but subtle was not one of them.

Barry dashed inside and did a quick recon. No one in the main gallery. Another door was bashed open at the farthest end of the room. While he'd been distracted by the Seven Deadly Tints, Roy Bivolo had managed to get pretty deep into Mega!

Beyond the busted interior door, Barry found a stairwell, which descended into darkness. A single light flickered down there, going from red to blue to yellow and back again.

The stairwell was tight, but it opened up at the bottom into a large basement. Crates lined the walls, storing artwork that the gallery had not yet displayed. Many of the crates had been ripped open, their tops broken and tossed aside, their contents rifled.

At the far end of the room stood Rainbow Raider, pawing through another crate. The flickering lights Barry had noticed earlier were coming from Bivolo's eyes as he searched the crate, then gave a triumphant cry and hoisted a framed canvas in the air, gazing at it.

Barry cleared his throat intentionally loudly. The sound echoed. Rainbow Raider spun around, still clutching the painting.

"Flash!"

"You know, after Kid Flash and I handed you your own butt last year, I figured you'd stay away from Central City," Barry taunted.

"You only defeated me because I made the mistake of teaming up with that loser Weather Wizard," Rainbow Raider snarled. "This time, *I'm* in charge."

"And it's going so well for you, too!" Barry exclaimed. "Your Seven Deadly Tints are already unconscious. Heck, the Central City Police Department has probably already started fingerprinting them. You're next."

"Really, Flash?" Rainbow Raider asked with a small grin. "Look into my eyes . . ."

Raider's power worked by locking eyes with his victims—he transmitted some kind of neural signal via the optic nerve, altering the subject's emotional state. Something to do with rebalancing hormones remotely. Barry hadn't heard the whole explanation from Caitlin because he'd already been in his suit and out the door when the call had come in. In any event, eye contact was important. And it was actually really difficult *not* to look in Bivolo's eyes. It was difficult not to look in *anyone's* eyes.

When you looked at someone, it was just where your own gaze naturally fell.

Rainbow Raider's eyes began to glow a sick and intense red. Barry acted quickly, thumbing a minute control in his glove. A set of slim, mirrored lenses slid down to cover the eyeholes in his mask, almost like a nictitating membrane. Birds, reptiles, and even some mammals had such membranes, which could be slid over the eye to protect it from dust without interfering with vision.

In Barry's case, it was a little more than dust that he needed protection from.

Just like that, Rainbow Raider's emotion-manipulating whammy reflected back on him. He dropped the canvas and shrieked with shock and outrage. Before the painting could hit the ground, Barry dashed over, caught it, and placed it gently on top of the crate. In the next tenth of a second, he slapped a set of S.T.A.R. Labs meta-dampening handcuffs on Rainbow Raider's wrists.

"You can't do this to me!" Bivolo howled.

"Check the tape; I already have." Barry took the Rogue by his elbow to lead him up the stairs and outside.

"I'm the victim!" Bivolo yelled, resisting. "I'm just taking back what's mine!"

Barry glanced over at the painting. The tragedy of Roy G. Bivolo's life had come long before the explosion of the

S.T.A.R. Labs particle accelerator granted him superpowers. It had begun at birth, or even earlier, when a chance defect in his photoreceptors caused massive damage to his fovea, the part of the eye that contained the highest concentration of cones and made color vision more vibrant and useful. Bivolo's fovea was severely deficient. His world wasn't quite black and white, but it definitely wasn't Technicolor.

This particular canvas depicted a lush landscape. The colors were all wrong—the grass a shade of red, the trees mottled blue and gray, the sky a greenish tint with pink clouds—and yet so great was the composition and so obvious the skill of the painter that it didn't matter. Roy Bivolo had the brush technique of Van Gogh and the eyesight of a Doberman.

"Someone got a bunch of my paintings from the police evidence lockup," Bivolo ranted, "and they're being sold on the black market. It's not right! These are *my* paintings! Mine!"

Barry hesitated just a moment, staring at the painting. It sure *looked* like an actual Bivolo. There was a minor market in Rainbow Raider counterfeits out there among the lower echelons of the art world, but Barry had taken some classes on art forgery in his capacity as a Central City Police CSI, and he prided himself on knowing the real deal when he saw it. This one looked legit, though he'd need to take it into the lab to be sure.

"If people are out there profiting off stolen police evidence, I'll be sure to stop them," he told Rainbow Raider. "In the meantime, it's off to Iron Heights for you."

He did, though, halfway to the stairs, turn one more time to look at the painting. At this distance, it was somehow even more beautiful.

What a waste of human potential. Barry sighed.

Outside, the crowd went wild when he emerged with Rainbow Raider in tow. Barry waved to them, enjoying the moment. If it went too far, he knew that he could tip all too easily into pure ego. But he had a job, he did it well, and he was anonymous—the occasional cheering crowd was the only reward he permitted himself. He banked the good feelings against darker and more lonesome days.

Joe West approached with a couple of CCPD uniformed officers. "Nice job, Flash," the detective said, taking Rainbow Raider away.

Pretending not to know his adoptive father, Barry nodded curtly. "Book him, Detective."

Joe's lips twitched for a moment into a knowing grin at Barry's faux seriousness. "Will do, Flash."

Barry waved to the crowd one more time and dashed away. He had hardly made it a block when his in-ear communicator buzzed.

"Flash, this is Home Base." It was Iris's voice in his ear. He couldn't suppress a smile. "I have Green Arrow on the line for you."

"Where's Vibe?" Barry asked. They were all trying to do a better job about using code names, even over their ultra-secure communications channel. Usually Cisco Ramon—Vibe—handled comms during super-villain battles.

"He's . . . communing. Arrow's getting impatient in my ear."

"Patch him through."

Barry hopped over a retaining wall and ran through Central City Park. It was the exact opposite of a shortcut—the route back to his lab at CCPD was shorter if he took the Cross-Central Expressway instead. But when you could move at the speed of light, it was no big deal to enjoy a scenic detour. Trees and bushes in the last full flower of summer whipped by, a swift panorama of greens, pinks, yellows, and reds.

He thought again of Bivolo's painting.

The next voice Barry heard was the gruff, no-nonsense tone of Oliver Queen.

"I need your help."

"Nice to talk to you, too. How's the wife?"

"This is serious," Green Arrow intoned.

"It always is." Barry leaped over a low hedge and skidded

around a corner. CCPD Headquarters slid into view before him. "What can I do for you?"

As Oliver spoke, Barry vibrated through an outer wall at CCPD, emerging in an empty staircase. While no one was around, he opened the Flash insignia ring he wore on his right hand. In an instant, the complicated futuristic tech inside the ring ionized his Flash costume, removing all of its nitrogen. The fabric reacted immediately to the lack of nitrogen, shrinking down to the size of a dime, which fit easily inside the ring, leaving Barry Allen in the staircase, wearing a pair of khakis and a slightly rumpled blue dress shirt. Oliver was still speaking in his earpiece.

". . . need to be able to keep an eye on all four buildings," he was saying. "At once."

Barry lifted his cell phone to his ear to pretend to be talking into it as he took the stairs two at a time. "Not a problem. I'll be there right after sunset. Is that cool?"

"Thanks, Barry." The relief in Oliver's voice was palpable, even over the wireless comms connection.

Upstairs in his lab, Barry was greeted by a scene of disarray. He'd been working on a tough case involving a pair of metahuman burglars who could read each other's minds and no one else's. They'd exploited this bizarre connection to form the world's most perfect crime duo, with one of them serving as lookout, able to communicate instantly to the other when there was danger. They didn't need cell phones—which could be hacked or tapped—or any other tech in order to coordinate their crimes.

Barry's job had been to prove that the two were in telepathic contact. Easier said than done! Telepathy by its very nature left no physical signs. So with the help of his friend Dr. Caitlin Snow at S.T.A.R. Labs, Barry had devised a series of tests that involved provoking one of the burglars while observing the other. He'd managed to prove a psychic connection when he shined a bright light into one crook's eyes and observed pupil dilation in the other.

The results of his many experiments were scattered around the lab. His boss, Captain David Singh, grudgingly tolerated Barry's comings and goings from work, as well as his general sloppiness, but there was no reason to irritate the captain unnecessarily. Barry took two seconds to clean up the lab, then settled in at his computer to type up his report.

He'd been working for maybe five minutes when he heard a cry go up from downstairs. Curious, he headed to the main staircase.

"She's *dead*!" a voice echoed up through the stairwell. A somewhat familiar voice. Where had he heard . . .

"Dead!" the voice cried out again, its tone anguished and agonized. It was a woman.

Barry jogged down the stairs. In the massive central

atrium of CCPD Headquarters, a group of cops had clustered.

From the center of the cluster came a high, keening wail, something half-mournful, half-pained. It sent a bolt of cold lightning down Barry's spine and made the fine hairs on the back of his neck stand up. He'd never heard something so wretched, so horrifying, and so sad in his life.

Joe was at the front of the cops. He had one hand on his holstered service weapon. Barry pushed his way over to Joe's side and finally beheld the person at the center of the group.

There, down on her knees, tears streaming down her face, rocking back and forth, fists clenched, was Madame Xanadu, wearing her usual peasant blouse, brocaded skirt, and brightly patterned head scarf.

Madame Xanadu. In an instant, memories flooded him: Entering her rickety old shop down on the Central City Pier. "Enter freely, and unafraid." The card deck that wasn't a Tarot deck but was unlike anything else he'd ever seen. Her admonition to him to "slow down," advice that had proved useful on more than one occasion when he'd fought Abra Kadabra, techno-mage from the future. The card she'd given him that had turned out to unlock the Spire of the Techno-Magicians in the sixty-fourth century. Her powers that—as much as the scientist in him hated to admit it— seemed like pure magic.

And more: Even in an entirely different universe, on the parallel world he called Earth 27, there'd been a version of Madame Xanadu, a doppelgänger who had somehow known his name and who he was.

It had been more than a year since he'd seen either of the Madame Xanadus, but he would never, ever forget her. Them. Whichever.

"Joe," Barry said in a low voice, "you don't need your gun."

Joe didn't divert attention from Madame Xanadu for an instant. "You know her?"

"Yeah." Barry flicked his attention around the circle. Especially in a town like Central City, continually beset by freaks, mutants, metahumans, and scientifically enhanced cretins of every stripe, the cops had itchy trigger fingers. He trusted Joe and most of the rest of the cops in the circle, but accidents could always happen.

He stepped into the circle and crouched down by Madame Xanadu. He took her hands in his own. Her strength was incredible as she clutched his hands like a life-line hurled from a distant shore.

"Dead! She's dead! No! No! What will we *do*?" She opened her tear-flooded eyes, and he saw stars in them, whirling and flashing lights that mesmerized him for a moment before he blinked rapidly and returned to reality.

"You're OK," he promised her. He tossed a reassuring look over his shoulder at the other cops, who relaxed visibly. "You're fine. Who's dead?"

She made a long, monosyllabic sound of disbelief, a sort of *nnnnnnnnnnnnnnn* that felt forever long. Shivering all over, she shook her head back and forth—whether denying him or her own thoughts, he couldn't tell.

Then, a moment of lucidity: She snapped her head forward, fixed his gaze with her own, and said, "Me. I am. *I'm* dead."

3

WITH CAPTAIN SINGH'S BLESSING, Barry transported Madame Xanadu to S.T.A.R. Labs. "There's a reason we have a contract with them," Singh said. "Let them earn that big fat retainer we pay them every month."

Joe helped Barry walk Madame Xanadu down to the garage, then stood lookout while Barry popped open his ring and slipped into the rapidly expanding Flash costume.

"Can you carry her all the way there?" Joe asked.

"She's pretty light," Barry said, slinging her over his shoulder in a fireman's carry. "And I've been working out."

After that single moment of lucidity, Madame Xanadu had relapsed. She alternated between babbling and outright screaming. Barry told S.T.A.R. that he was on his way and ran.

The S.T.A.R. Labs building looked something like an upside-down stool with only three legs—massive pylons jutting out from the circular main structure. It was a hub of super-science, the place where Barry and his team worked to keep the world and the universe safe from harm.

By the time he got to the lab, overlooking the river, his shoulders burned with exertion and strain. It was funny—running at Mach 4 didn't make his legs hurt, but carrying a hundred pounds of deadweight was torture. Such were the vagaries of the speed force—if something didn't relate to moving fast, his body reacted like anyone else's.

The Cortex was the hub of S.T.A.R. Labs. It boasted a series of workstations with high-end computer gear, all of it tied in to the big monitors arranged around the room. Years ago, when the facility had been a research lab dedicated to the creation and study of dark matter, the Cortex had been its nerve center, where Harrison Wells and his team of intrepid mad scientists controlled and monitored the experiments.

Up until the big one. The explosion of the particle accelerator had cast a wave of dark matter over the city. That dark matter interacted with certain people, imbuing them with superpowers, and suddenly a fusillade of metahumans launched into an unsuspecting world.

"We weren't really mad scientists," Cisco had once said. "More like slightly perturbed."

Nowadays, S.T.A.R. Labs' accelerator was permanently decommissioned and off-line. The building itself served as the headquarters for Team Flash, and the Cortex was where they ran their operations.

Iris was at the communications board when Barry skidded to a halt. She had been a reporter for a while, using her contacts and her journalistic acumen to help hunt down bad guys. But shortly after the wedding, she'd left that job and come to S.T.A.R. Labs full-time, serving as a coordinator and also generally running relations between the lab and the various city agencies that relied on it. Married people were supposed to be partners, and she and Barry were partners in everything: work, life, love.

Iris usually had a big, open smile for Barry, but not today. She swept her hair out of her eyes and pressed her lips together in concern as she watched him gently lower Madame Xanadu into a nearby chair. Madame Xanadu had gone silent during the second-long superspeed run from CCPD and now stared into the distance, seeing things no one else could, captivated by whatever demons haunted her.

Demons. For all Barry knew, it was literal in her case.

"Dead dead dead dead . . ." she moaned, a line of drool snaking its way down her jawline.

Caitlin rushed over from the medical bay. "What the . . . Barry, who *is* this?"

"Meet Madame Xanadu."

Now Iris gasped and joined them. "*The* Madame Xanadu?"

"The one and only." Barry thought about Earth 27. "Well, in a manner of speaking."

They watched as Caitlin performed a quick initial examination of Madame Xanadu, shining a flashlight into the moaning woman's eyes to check for pupillary response. Those eyes, moments ago star-filled, reverted to normal as Madame Xanadu relaxed the tiniest bit under Caitlin's care. Caitlin Snow was one of the world's top physicians, with a healthy dose of schooling in the finer arts of super-science as well. She was compassionate and beyond competent—if she couldn't heal it, it couldn't be healed.

"What's wrong with her?" Caitlin asked.

"I was hoping you could tell me," Barry said. Iris took his hand and squeezed. Barry was once again grateful for his wife. She truly understood how mystifying and important Madame Xanadu was to him. The boardwalk seer had appeared to him as though conjured by need during his darkest hour. The evil techno-wizard from the future, Abra Kadabra, had used his future science to enthrall Barry, and Madame Xanadu had provided the key to Barry's liberation, saving him from a life of eternal servitude.

Then when he was lost on Earth 27, her doppelgänger there had pointed him in the right direction, leading him to a coterie of allies and a way to defeat the evil speedster Johnny Quick.

She had vanished, though, and he'd never even been able to thank her. Maybe now that she was the one in dire straits . . . Maybe now he could repay his debt.

Caitlin gnawed at her bottom lip as she jotted down some notes on Madame Xanadu's condition. "Her blood pressure is sky-high, and her pulse is racing. Pupils shrinking but reactive. I'm saying it's shock, but it's the worst I've ever seen. Barry, down in the medical supply, there's a rack of green ampoules in the cabinet marked SEDATIVES. Can you get me—"

He was already back with a handful of them. Caitlin chuckled. "I only needed one," she said. Barry Flashed the rest of them back and was at Caitlin's side before she'd even injected Madame Xanadu.

"This will take the edge off and help her rest," Caitlin said. As they watched, Madame Xanadu's breathing slowed and her eyelids fluttered. She didn't quite fall asleep, but she slumped in the chair, her eyes mere slits, her respiration now even and calm.

"Where's Cisco?" Barry asked Iris. He couldn't forget that Madame Xanadu had—while talking and breathing— said that she herself was already dead. Sounded like delusion, yes, but in Barry's world it could also be time travel, dimension hopping, or just plain weird science. And when it came to weird science, Cisco was his first call.

"Downstairs," Iris said. "Still . . . communing." Her face clouded over as she said it. Barry knew why.

"None of it is about us," he told her, taking her hands. "None of it is your fault. Look, why don't you help Caitlin get Madame Xanadu settled into the medical bay?"

Iris nodded, touched his arm briefly, and then helped Caitlin get Madame Xanadu into a wheelchair and out the door.

"Mis amigos!" Cisco strolled into the Cortex, passing the three women on his way. His hair, long and lustrous, was tied back in a ponytail, a look that made his face seem more mature somehow. "I've returned! How goes it?"

"You tell me," Barry replied. "What's up in TV land?"

A year or so ago, Cisco had stumbled upon a shocking and existentially fraught secret—there was another timeline, nearly identical to their own.

It wasn't a parallel Earth—it was an entire timeline with a Multiverse of its own, a slightly twisted mirror image of their reality, "an identical twin with a different haircut," as Joe had once described it. It was so big a discovery that they'd had to invent some new terminology. After much debate, Cisco (of course) came up with "transmultiversal version," which they often just shortened to "TV" for convenience's sake.

There were as many similarities between their world and the TV world as there were differences. In each reality, there'd been an invasion of super-Nazis from Earth-X that had been turned back. In each reality, Barry and Iris had wed, as had their friends Oliver and Felicity. They'd even fought some of the same villains.

But TV-Barry's creation and negation of Flashpoint had had a ripple effect, causing some dramatic differences between the two timelines. As best they could tell, the TV crew had never faced villains like Blue Bolt, the Living Hashtag, Major Disaster, or the Construct. Cisco's brother Dante was dead "over there." Caitlin had a Killer Frost split personality.

And their friend H.R. Wells, from Earth 19, had sacrificed his life in the other timeline to save Iris. Shortly after they learned this, their own H.R. had left S.T.A.R. Labs for good to explore, to find both himself and his place in the world.

TV-H.R.'s death hit Iris particularly hard, since it had been to protect her TV version. Barry kept reminding her that what happened in the other timeline didn't impact them here in theirs . . . and that the opposite was also true. Nothing she had done here had caused the other H.R.'s death.

Every few months, the two Ciscos used their vibe powers to make contact with each other and catch each other up on happenings in the different timelines. It was so far the only way they'd discovered to communicate between the two realities.

"Same old, same old," Cisco replied. "Fast people, cool costumes, bad guys who need a punch in the jaw."

"Has their Cisco told his Team Flash about our existence yet?"

Cisco hesitated for a moment, then shook his head, shaking his ponytail back and forth. "No. He still thinks it's a bad idea to tell them."

Barry frowned. "Keeping secrets—"

"We can't judge them," Cisco said hurriedly. "They've had a rough time over there. Over then. There? Then? I don't know. Anyway: They had that whole Savitar mess that we never went through, and then they had a *really* tough time with the Thinker."

Barry was bemused. "The Thinker? Really?"

The Thinker—Clifford Devoe, an insane and brilliant college professor who'd plotted to rule the world by making everyone else in it incredibly stupid—had been defeated about a year ago by Team Flash. At first, they'd been flummoxed by his ability to predict their every move. But then H.R., of all people, had come up with a solution.

"If he can predict what you're doing," H.R. had said, knocking back a cup of extremely hot, extremely strong, extremely expensive coffee, "then be unpredictable."

It was easier said than done because the Thinker could process every conceivable outcome and figure out the most likely one. So Cisco had come up with the Schrödinger Cage that he built into Barry's suit. Erwin Schrödinger was a physicist who had developed a way of explaining quantum superposition, the idea that physical objects could be in two states at once. Famously, he asked people to imagine a cat in a box. Also inside the box was a packet of poison. There was a fifty-fifty chance of the packet opening, thereby killing the cat. But until someone actually opened the box, there was no way to know if the cat was alive or dead. Until the box was opened, then, the cat was both alive *and* dead, existing in a state of "quantum uncertainty" until someone observed it.

The Schrödinger Cage operated on an expansion of this principle. It put Barry's atoms into quantum superposition so that he was in multiple places at once, causing multiple interactions at the same time. Devoe could defend against what he could predict . . . but not when his predictions were mutually exclusive. Thanks to the Schrödinger Cage, Barry's potential actions had canceled each other out, and Devoe had been helpless. Right now, the Thinker occupied a power-dampening cell at Iron Heights, where he was no smarter than any other college professor.

"There's more," Cisco went on. "Stuff about your daughter . . ." At Barry's shocked look, he chuckled. "Don't go shopping for a pregnancy test yet, you dog. It's all time travel stuff. Anyway . . . They seem to be doing OK over there now, and we're doing fine, so I'm happy to announce that all's well in two different realities. That's gotta be a record."

Barry nodded thoughtfully. It wasn't easy to put TV out of his mind, but he had to. It didn't impact his life at all, but the mere knowledge of it throbbed like a bad tooth. Through Kid Flash, he'd asked the time-traveling Legends to look into the alternate timeline. He just wanted to keep a weather eye on it. So far, there seemed to be no consequences of the split his alternate version had caused, but he wanted to be sure. In his world and in his experience, trouble could come from almost any direction.

"I want you to vibe something for me," Barry said, changing the topic.

Cisco made a show of cracking his knuckles and proceeded to blow imaginary dust off his fingertips. "These magical digits," he said, waggling his fingers, "are at your disposal."

• • •

Caitlin crossed her arms over her chest and cocked her hip, standing in front of Madame Xanadu's bed to block Barry and Cisco. "I'm not letting you get those grubby vibe hands anywhere near my patient," she said.

Barry and Cisco exchanged a look of bafflement. "Caitlin!" Cisco cried out. "Buddy! Pal! C'mon! This is what we *do* here at Team Flash."

"Not today. I don't know what this woman has experienced or what kind of meta she is. I'm not risking it."

Barry held his hands up to placate her. "I get it. You're being protective. And normally that's great. But she's in a lot of distress, and this is the only way we can help her."

Meanwhile, Cisco was studying his hands. "Grubby?" he mouthed.

Caitlin shook her head. "We wait for her to regain her senses. To give consent to have Cisco vibe her. That's the right thing to do. The ethical thing to do."

"She might not regain her senses," Barry said. "Not entirely. You hit her with a sedative, but she's still awake." Sure enough, in her bed, Madame Xanadu was moaning softly, her eyes half-open. Her fingers clenched and unclenched over and over. "What if she's getting worse? Or what if she's like this forever and we could have helped her?"

"With my incredibly *clean* hands," Cisco said, a bit miffed. "I mean, I had a manicure, like, two days ago."

Caitlin flicked her eyes back and forth between Barry and Madame Xanadu. Finally, she relented. "OK. But right now, her vitals are stable. If her blood pressure starts to spike or her heart rate jumps, I will personally tackle Cisco to break contact."

Cisco's eyebrows arched. "For real? Do I need my football pads?"

"Just do it," Caitlin said, "before I change my mind."

She stepped aside, and Cisco approached the side of the bed. He hesitated for a moment, glancing back at Barry. Barry shrugged and looked over at Caitlin, who nodded, then turned her attention to the medical monitor attached to Madame Xanadu.

Cisco reached out and touched Madame Xanadu's bare arm with the tips of all ten fingers.

And

something

exploded

inside him, inside his mind his

brain his very core oh wow oh

God something like a rainbow made of lightning and then swirling broken shards of stars and sunlight and shadows made of rain and a mirror that could not look back and a spinning disk made of tears and and and and

"Cisco?"

Voice. From somewhere. Somewhere else. Familiar. Barry. Friend.

Cisco gritted his teeth. He leaned into the vibe. What was he *seeing*?

It was like watching a thousand TV channels at once. It was like having a fly's vision, witnessing the world through a compound eye. Except each facet was different. Not a new angle on the same thing, but a different view entirely, each "screen" a wholly unique visual and experience. He couldn't keep them all straight in his head.

A candy shop.

A rocket, blasting off.

An endless desert of dirty white sand, clouds scudding overhead like filth floating atop stagnant water.

And then . . .

No, impossible. The perspective was all wrong . . .

He was looking up at a blood-red sky, cut and slashed by jagged bolts of black lightning. Red rain fell in sheets, as though the sky itself were bleeding. And there, among the shock and clash of lightning, barely perceptible through the haze, he thought he saw . . .

No. No! That just *couldn't* be!

But it was. The sky itself was torn open. Like one of his breaches, but instead of being circular and contained, with a gently blurred circumference, this was a vicious gash across the sky. Ragged edges along the miles-tall tear. Where his breaches seemed almost gentle and unobtrusive, this one was a violent, savage rupture in the fabric of reality itself.

And within . . . Someone . . . A man . . .

"Cisco?"

He leaned forward, peering through the storm, trying to see, trying to understand . . .

And that's when the visions dissolved, the vibe broken, the medical bay at S.T.A.R. Labs melting back into place around him. He'd been knocked to the floor, his connection to Madame Xanadu severed. Barry stood over him, a look of concern on his face.

"What the H-E-double hockey sticks, Barry?" Cisco ranted. "I was almost there! I was getting it, and you knock me down?"

Barry shook his head. "I had to. You weren't listening to me."

"Your whole body was seizing." This from Caitlin, who was crouched next to him, slipping a blood pressure cuff over his left arm. "We couldn't let you stay in the vibe. It was too intense."

"I'm fine." He tried to shake off the cuff but was surprised to find that his entire body was shaking and only barely under his control.

"Your adrenaline spiked," Caitlin told him. "You were gripping Madame Xanadu's arm so tightly that I thought you were going to cut off her circulation."

"What did you see?" Barry asked, holding out a hand. He and Caitlin helped Cisco to his feet, then supported him and assisted him into a nearby chair.

Cisco pinched the bridge of his nose, closed his eyes, and took a deep breath. As best he could, he described what he'd seen. As he focused to recollect, he realized something: He'd been seeing multiple Earths all at once, through the prism of Madame Xanadu.

"She has Multiversal awareness," he whispered.

At Barry's and Caitlin's perplexed looks, he explained: "Madame Xanadu is somehow connected to every other version of herself in the Multiverse. They each have each other's memories and they can see through each other's eyes, experience each other's realities. Fifty-two of them, all synchronized and running the same operating system."

"Fifty-*one* of them," Barry said quietly.

Cisco frowned with his eyebrows, then realized. *She's dead!* Madame Xanadu had cried out. One of her alternates had died. That's what she meant.

"The psychic kickback sent her into a sort of existential shock," Caitlin opined. "I don't even know where to begin medically because—"

"He's coming," Madame Xanadu said, sitting upright in bed. Her eyes were blank and unseeing, her affect slack, her voice toneless. "He's coming."

And she collapsed back onto the bed again.

Barry stared straight ahead. Caitlin cleared her throat and said nothing.

Cisco sighed. "They never mean the pizza guy when they say that."

4

OLIVER PERCHED HIGH ATOP THE
Aparo Tower, roughly a block away from the
barricaded no-man's-land that had once been
the Glades. Star City had the beauty of a cobra. It was
deadly and hypnotic all at once, and he had to admit that he
wouldn't have it any other way. He liked his city somewhat
mysterious—he just wanted it to be better and more fair
at the same time.

He'd grown up here, the wealthy scion of the city's
leading family. He knew best the shining tops of towers and
the mansions of the most exclusive districts, but he loved
every inch of Star City, from the broken sidewalks to the
highest penthouses. That the city still hadn't rebuilt after
the devastation of the Glades was a source of shame for him,

though he knew too well the niggling practicalities that had kept the construction equipment from moving in. There were zoning ordinances and contract bids to sort through, architectural details and city planning standards . . . He was wealthy and politically connected, and he'd been pushing as hard as he could to rebuild the city, but some things took their own time.

Not every problem could be solved with a mask, a voice modulator, and an arrow through the center of the bull's-eye.

More's the pity, he thought, turning his attention away from the Glades and to the buildings nearby.

He'd chosen the rooftop of the Aparo Tower not because it was the tallest building in the vicinity—it wasn't—but rather because it was the perfect vantage point from which to observe the four buildings Felicity had identified as the most likely targets for their serial bomber. He had his team staked out closer to each individual building. Spartan—his former bodyguard and current right-hand man, John Diggle—was watching one while Wild Dog— Rene Ramirez, street-scrapper extraordinaire—was parked a block up from the second building on his motorcycle, ready to roll. Mr. Terrific—Curtis Holt—was monitoring the third building with his incredibly high-tech T-spheres, and Black Canary—Dinah Drake, possessor of the fierce Canary Cry—had eyes on the fourth building.

For himself, Oliver had chosen the angel seat, the over-arching holistic position. He could see all four buildings and have his team move at a moment's notice.

Bird's-eye view whenever possible, his frenemy and mentor Slade Wilson had taught him. *All the better to swoop down on your enemies.*

Oliver sighed. He'd been all about swooping down on his enemies once. He'd had a list of people who'd done wrong, and he had been determined to go down that list one by one and eliminate each of them from the face of the earth. But now he was more interested in justice than vengeance.

It wasn't about retribution anymore. If he had to let the bad guy go in order to save lives, so be it.

Better not to have to make the choice, right?

The sun had set about twenty minutes ago, and Star City was steeped in early autumn darkness. It was chilly up here on the rooftop, but the thermal layers in his Green Arrow costume kept him warm, preventing his muscles from locking up, keeping him limber. He resisted the urge to check the time. Barry had promised he would be here, and looking at the time every thirty seconds wasn't going to get him here any faster.

Off in the distance, a burst of light flickered for an instant on the horizon. Lightning? He glanced up at the sky. It was a clear night. No rain in the forecast. That meant . . .

"Hey, Oliver!"

He spun around, fighting every instinct in his body to nock an arrow. There on the rooftop stood none other than Barry Allen, the Flash. Sparks of electricity still winkled in the air around him, coruscating tidbits of lightning from the channeling of the mysterious Speed Force.

"Took you long enough to get here," Oliver said. "And remember: code names. We're in the field."

Barry looked around. "Riiiiiight. Because someone might be wandering around on the rooftop and overhear me."

Oliver grunted.

"And I'm not late. I'm right on time." He tapped the left side of his mask, and Oliver imagined him receiving some sort of information feed. "Oh. OK, so I'm late. Oops. Sorry. There's drama back home."

"When is there not?"

Barry came over to Oliver's side, standing tall and obvious in his bright red-and-yellow suit. Oliver gritted his teeth. "Could you not be so . . . overt?"

As though he'd just realized, Barry looked down at Oliver. "Have you even moved in the last few hours?" Barry asked. "Because deep vein thrombosis is a thing, Oliver. I worry about you, always crouching on rooftops."

"We've identified four possible targets," Oliver told him, ignoring the medical advice. He pointed out the buildings.

"There, there, there, and there. We think the bomber will go after one of them."

"With something like this, you mean?" Barry asked innocently, holding out a rather sophisticated explosive device.

Oliver blinked. He was constantly caught off guard by Barry's speed. He *knew* the Flash was fast. He *knew* Barry Allen could race lightning bolts and win, could flick on a light switch and then unscrew the bulb before it turned on. But knowing that and seeing it in action were two separate things, and as much as he would never admit it to Barry, it was often pretty unnerving to witness the fruits of that incredible speed.

"You found that . . ." he began.

"In the fourth building," Barry admitted. "It's always the last place you look, am I right?" He hefted the device. "This thing is impressive, I have to say. I've disarmed a lot of explosives in my days with CCPD, but this one is special. Redundant kill switches tied in to multiple redundant signaling paths . . . And some really expertly applied fake wires that go nowhere and do nothing, but *look* like they do something."

"To slow down a Bomb Disposal Unit," Oliver said. "Making it less likely someone could disarm the thing before it went off."

"It *did* slow me down," Barry said, handing the thing over. "It took me an extra tenth of a second to disarm it. Good thing I'm a cop *and* a speedster, right?"

Oliver accepted the bomb, holding it somewhat gingerly. It wasn't that he didn't trust Barry's skills—it was just that the thing was still a bomb, deactivated or not. He looked down at it. This device—more accurately, ones just like it—had taken down three buildings in his city. Caused untold property damage. Spiked the fear of an entire city.

He was impressed by what Barry had done, but that didn't matter right now. What mattered was what came next. "Did you disturb the scene at all?" he demanded. Barry was fast but sometimes sloppy. All that speed made little things like caution, delicacy, and precision seem trivial. "We need evidence if we're going to track this guy down and put him away for good."

Under his cowl, Barry's expression was offended. "What did I just say? I'm a cop." He held up his other hand, producing a standard-issue CSI evidence collection kit. The seal was broken, meaning he'd opened it up and used what was inside. "While I was grabbing the bomb, I also took the liberty of dusting for prints and collecting soil and fiber samples. I also cordoned off the room so that you can go through it and take pictures." He frowned. "I move so fast that cameras can't keep up. Speed of light isn't fast enough, you know? Anyway, I basically did a complete evidence workup on the scene for you."

Oliver accepted the evidence kit and signaled Mr. Terrific and Spartan to move in on the building in question to take photos and do a secondary evidence sweep. "You make it too easy sometimes," he mock-complained to Barry.

Barry grinned. "Nah. It *should* be easy."

Despite himself, Oliver grinned back. All the tension and built-up anxiety that had tautened his entire body bled out of him. He stood, tucked the bomb and evidence kit under one arm, and offered his hand to the Flash. "Thanks, Barry." Blessed relief flooded in, replacing the fleeing dread. There would be no explosion tonight. No wreckage and debris. No more fear toxins dumped into the city like fertilizer into a garden of terror.

Pumping Oliver's hand, Barry widened his smile. "No problem. Always glad to help out, like last year, that thing with Ricardo Diaz."

Oliver nodded knowingly. Ricardo Diaz had been a drug lord and crime boss who'd targeted Star City for a takeover. Fortunately, Barry had wrapped up his own difficulties with the Thinker in time to run over from Central City and lend a hand.

"That could have played out much differently," Oliver acknowledged. "I might have even ended up in jail. Thanks for your help then and now."

"That's what friends are—" Barry stiffened and put a hand to his right earpiece. "What did you say?" he asked.

Oliver watched his friend's expression. Even with the concealment of the mask, there was still enough of Barry's face exposed that he could read the worry that crawled there. The Flash costume also didn't hide the eyes, and those eyes were now staring into the distance, jittering back and forth in distress. Someone at S.T.A.R. Labs was giving Barry either very bad or very shocking news. Maybe both.

"Oliver," Barry said, his voice trembling, "I have to—"

"Go," Oliver commanded, and the syllable hadn't even left his mouth when a blast of wind and a crackle of electricity erupted all around him.

He spun around and watched the Flash's lightning trail blaze down the side of the Aparo Tower and then up Jerome Boulevard, heading east. Central City was six hundred miles away, but Oliver knew that by the time he finished inhaling his latest breath, Barry Allen would be more than halfway home.

Breach . . . Speedsters . . . Panic . . .

The words reverberated in Barry's memory as he ran from Star City to Central City. Usually when he made these jaunts, he checked out the scenery and took little split-second detours into the towns along the way, just to help out however he could. Stopping a mugging here, getting a dog out of a sewer grate there . . . All at invisible superspeed, never stopping for applause or acknowledgment. When you could move as fast as he could, the difference between stopping to help out and not stopping was mere seconds at most. It was always worth it.

But right now, he was a bullet on a straight-line path for Central City, with no time for sightseeing or side trips.

"There's a breach!" Iris had told him, her voice rising and near-frenzied. *"Right in the middle of the city! Speedsters everywhere! Panic in the streets! Get home now!"*

For the Flash, *now* was never more than a minute away from anywhere else on the planet. Barry cruised into Central City no more than forty seconds after leaving Green Arrow's side.

And did something he rarely did when in costume: Stopped. Dead. In. His. Tracks.

Iris hadn't been exaggerating. Half a block north of the intersection of Kanigher Avenue and Heck Street, a truly massive breach yawned wide open, its edges crackling with a malign energy. Black bubbles sizzled along its circumference, popping, recombining, popping again. The air smelled like ozone and magma. CCPD was out in force, trying to manage the panic, but the police were overwhelmed. Barry glanced around and spotted Joe West among the cops, shouting out orders and directing the foot traffic onto side streets. Streetlights illuminated the scene in a lurid glow, throwing shadows against walls and the ground as people ran.

Central Citizens fled pell-mell from the breach, climbing over stalled cars, scrambling for cover behind newspaper boxes, large concrete planters, and benches. In and among them were hundreds—maybe thousands—of people moving *way* too fast to be mere humans.

Thousands of speedsters. And more of them streaming out of the breach by the second, scurrying about in obvious terror, throwing horrified glances over their shoulders as they went.

Barry squinted, gazing into the breach, trying to see what they were running *from* . . .

And he spotted it. There, far, *far* back in the breach, he could just barely make out . . . something. A figure, vaguely humanoid. A massive, towering form, calmly walking toward the breach from whatever world was on the other side. It had to be huge to be seen and identified at this distance. At least three hundred feet tall, maybe more. Barry's mind reeled at the sheer scale of it. Something that big . . . How could it even exist?

"Look!" someone shouted, his voice trembling with outright terror. "Up in the sky!"

Barry shifted his gaze. At the very top of the enormous breach, three figures had emerged, flying under their own power. One was a woman in a deep blue leotard and a white cape, twirling a sparkling, golden lasso. Her eyes flashed with malign intent, her lips twisted into a cruel smile. The way she scanned the crowd below sent a shiver down Barry's spine—it was like watching a lion consider which gazelle to sink its teeth into.

Another was a slender man in a green-and-black skintight outfit with a green domino mask. His entire body was enfolded in a glowing green sheath of energy. He seemed somewhat confused, but not in an innocent or naive way—it was the confusion of a bully, of someone who punches his way out of misunderstandings.

The last was the most frightening of all. He was a muscular figure in blue tights and a red cape with a red *U* emblazoned on his chest, and his expression was of complete contempt and utter disregard. If the woman was a lion ready to eat its prey, this guy was a kid with a mean streak about to shove a firecracker into an anthill for absolutely no reason at all. And the anthill was Barry's city.

That red *U* was familiar, though. Barry thought about it for just an instant, rifling through his memory . . .

It came to him: Earth 27. He'd been trapped there a year or so ago. It was a world where good guys were evil and bad guys were good. The James Jesse of that world had taken him in and told him how Earth 27 was controlled by a group of metahumans called the Crime Syndicate of America. He'd seen the symbols for the various members on a map, and this red *U* was one of them.

Ultraman, that was the guy's name. Which meant the woman was Superwoman. And the other guy was either Power Ring or Owlman.

Which further meant that . . . the speedsters all around, causing so much chaos and confusion, were the people from Earth 27's Central City. Barry had taught Johnny Quick's speed formula to James Jesse and told him to spread the word. It had spread pretty far, apparently.

Barry had run out of time. Even thinking as fast as he did, time had passed, and he had to do *something*. Now. He took off from a standing start, accelerating beyond the speed of sound almost effortlessly. He started moving people out of harm's way, away from the breach and out of the path of the rampaging stampede of panicked speedsters.

"Something's happened on Earth 27," he barked into his communicator. He was talking too quickly for anyone to understand him—his voice would just sound like one long, uninterrupted, high-pitched squeal—but Cisco had rigged up some equipment on the other end of the communicator that slowed down his speech for human ears. "They're evacuating right onto our Earth. We need crowd control ASAP. Plus, we need some super-villain wrangling. Call Star City and tell Green Arrow it's time to pay me back for the favor I just did him."

5

IN THE BUNKER, OLIVER WATCHED WITH detached amusement as John Diggle paced back and forth, gesticulating wildly with both hands. Everything about Dig was big—his hands, his shoulders, his gestures. And his mood. John Diggle—the hero known as Spartan— couldn't hide his joys, his pains, his worries. And right now, he couldn't hide his exasperation.

"It's not that I don't *like* the guy," Dig was saying. "I do. I like him a lot. I'm just saying that when he does stuff like this, I sort of go, 'Hey, why bother being human? What good are we?' And I know he doesn't do it on *purpose*, but when you can move that fast, maybe slow down every now and then and let us mere mortals achieve something."

"Right." Oliver leaned back on a bank of computers

and folded his arms over his chest. "Let a couple of buildings blow up so that we can feel good about ourselves."

"Exactly!" Dig shouted in triumph, then realized what
he'd just said. "That's not what I meant and you know it."

"It's a different world out there than the one you and I
started in all those years ago," Oliver told him. "Sometimes
I feel like we're cavemen compared to guys like him, but we
have something important to offer."

"Cannon fodder?" Dig joked bleakly.

"Hardly. We're the thinkers. The planners. And we're
the ones who remember that even when everyone is
jumping around the Multiverse, there are actual *people* at
risk. People who matter. People who can't leap tall buildings or travel through time. Sometimes, with all the
superpowers flying around, it's too easy to get caught up
in winning the fight, and we forget what we're fighting for.
For *them.* For the people who can't hurl lightning bolts or
walk through walls. We do it for them, and we are living
reminders of that."

Dig pursed his lips, considering, then gave a slow,
thoughtful nod.

"Hard to make science with all the pontificating going
on!" Curtis Holt said from his workstation. Slender and
intense, with a lanky, energetic vibe, Curtis had joined
Felicity at one of the Bunker's worktables, where they

hunched over to examine the bomb the Flash had recovered. They'd meticulously disassembled it down to its raw components and now were painstakingly identifying a chain of ownership for each piece, trying to determine how it had been built . . . and by whom.

"Just keeping it real," Dig told him.

"As he said," Oliver said equably.

"Could you keep it *down* while you're keeping it real?" Felicity snapped, engrossed in a microscopic component. She gave a little gasp and flipped up the microzoom goggles she was wearing. "I meant to say," she said sweetly, "could you keep it down, *my dear husband, light of my life?*"

Oliver chuckled dryly. "How long are you two going to be pawing through that tech? Maybe Dig and I'll grab Rene and go get some dinn—"

He broke off as the Bunker filled with a loud, piercing shriek; red lights pulsated overhead. Dig's hand went for his weapon, but Oliver waved him off.

"That's the Flash's emergency beacon. He's never used it before."

Just then, the main monitor flickered to life. Iris West-Allen loomed over them all. "Team Arrow! Sorry to break in like this . . ."

"That's why we installed the system in the first place," Oliver told her. "What's up?"

"Barry says—and I quote—'Time for Green Arrow to pay back that favor I just did for him.' We've got a Multiversal breach in the middle of the city, a bunch of panicked speedsters running around, *and* at least three people with the power of flight and the power of bad attitudes. Can you guys lend a hand?"

Oliver turned to look at Dig, who'd already grabbed his Spartan gear off a nearby rack. "Felicity . . ."

She nodded curtly, all business. "Take Curtis and Rene with you. Grab Dinah, too. I'll stay here and work on the bomb stuff."

"Are you sure?" he asked. "Maybe Curtis could stay."

She shook her head firmly. "They're going to need all the help they can get. Go."

Oliver snatched up his bow. "Suit up and roll out!" he said.

"It should totally be called the Arrowplane," said Curtis Holt as he strapped into the pilot's seat.

"We're not calling it the Arrowplane!" Oliver yelled from the main cabin.

They were a hundred feet underground in a concealed launch facility that had once been a Queen Industries subway extension project. The project had been shuttered when the Glades sank into the bowels of the earth, and Oliver had repurposed the facility, figuring it would come in handy someday. Now it was a massive, hangar-sized space with an elevator as tall as most skyscrapers.

Curtis Holt was one of the smartest, most accomplished human beings alive, with doctorates in more than a dozen fields of study. He had lived up to his code name—Mr. Terrific—and done some, well, terrific work down in the hangar. He'd built a supersonic jet capable of vertical takeoff like a rocket, needing no runway space. It could jump into the upper reaches of the atmosphere and cut a parabolic arc over the curvature of Earth, letting it traverse great distances in incredibly brief amounts of time. It wasn't quite Flash-level speed, but it was the next best thing.

Curtis was in the pilot's seat, with Dig next to him. In the back was Oliver, of course, along with Dinah Drake— the Black Canary—and Rene Ramirez, Wild Dog.

"Is this more superhero junk, hoss?" Rene asked. He was more at home with the street-level justice at which he excelled. Super-stuff felt perpetually out of his league. When Oliver first met him, he'd been armed with nothing more than a few guns and a suit of homemade "armor" that included a hockey goalie's mask. Now he was decked out with serious tech, but he remained a street brawler at heart.

"It's going to be fine," Oliver said, double-checking the buckles on his restraints. They'd never actually flown the plane before—it was still technically an experiment.

A beta product, Curtis called it. There was a slight chance they'd all blow up on takeoff.

"It goes up in the air," Curtis was saying, "and then arcs and comes down. Like an arrow shot into the sky. So: Arrowplane."

"Not. Calling it. Arrowplane," Oliver insisted. "Just get us to Central City."

Curtis shrugged and flipped some switches. "Engaging main thrusters. Felicity, do you read me?"

"Read you." Felicity's voice crackled through the speakers. "I show nothing in your flight path. You're cleared for launch, Arrowplane."

"It's not—!"

Oliver's protest was swallowed by a thunderous, crashing roar as Mr. Terrific engaged the thrusters. The ceiling yawned open as the ground shook and the plane vibrated all around them. And then, in an instant, they were airborne, blasting over the horizon, heading east toward Central City.

6

NEARLY OUT OF BREATH, BARRY paused for half a second at the event horizon of the breach. Here, the imbalance of atmospheric pressure between Earth 1 and Earth 27 caused a foul wind to blow in from the parallel world. It carried the stench of death, of scorched brick, of something else he couldn't identify but which made his fingers tremble. Even the *light* on Earth 27 looked different, corrupted, decaying. And there was still that figure, so far away yet so threatening, so huge, moving relentlessly forward.

Barry had spent the last half hour moving people out of harm's way and trying to corral the speedsters. They weren't evil or even merely bad; they were just average, frightened people with a superpower. Fortunately, most of them were on the slow end of fast. None of them could even get close to Mach 1. Barry was able to round a bunch of them up and point them to the best evacuation routes. With speedsters leading the way, people were now moving in a more orderly fashion up Kanigher, then splitting and heading for the safety of uptown along Larocque and Lampert Streets.

Up above, Ultraman and Power Ring were beating the snot out of each other. Barry thanked his lucky stars that these guys apparently didn't have the brains to go with their incredible powers—he'd tricked them into colliding with each other while they were trying to zap *him*, and now they were zapping each other instead. Ultraman's eyes blazed a sickly red and beams of heat vision lashed the sky, narrowly missing Power Ring. Ultraman seemed to have all the Kryptonian powers of Barry's friend Kara—Supergirl—from Earth 38. Barry had no desire to tussle with *that* kind of power.

The other guy, Power Ring, lived up to his name. He wore a green ring on his right hand that flashed and flared and seemed to conjure whatever he could imagine. Fortunately, Power Ring's imagination seemed to be severely limited. He was just firing blasts at Ultraman and whipping up shields for himself. If he *really* understood the power of that ring, Barry thought with a shudder, it would be all over. With that kind of power at his disposal, he could—

"Urk!" Barry's hands flew up to his throat, clawing there. He'd been caught out, and now Superwoman's glowing lasso was wrapped around his neck, choking him.

She tightened her grip and yanked him closer to her; he stumbled over on legs gone weak from constant, uninterrupted running. Her lips curled into a cruel smile. "My mystical lasso makes you my slave, little runner. I never managed to get it around Johnny Quick, but now I have a pet speedster, just like I always wanted." Her smile ratcheted up a notch. "Assuming I don't just kill you, that is. That's always been my problem: I keep killing the men who should be serving me."

As Barry struggled for breath, he flashed back to more than a year ago. Abra Kadabra—then going by the name Hocus Pocus—had come to the twenty-first century from the sixty-fourth with the express purpose of killing the famous Flash. To start, he'd used his nanotechnology to make Barry his puppet, controlling his every move and action. For the first time in his life since becoming the Flash, Barry had been completely helpless, utterly unable to fight back for himself or for the people he'd sworn to protect. It had been a nightmare, a painful, terrifying part of Barry's life, and there was no way in the world he was going to relive it at the hands of this Earth 27 psychopath.

He tried vibrating through the lasso, but something in its composition absorbed and counterbalanced his vibrations.

He remained depressingly solid, and oxygen was becoming a scarce commodity in his lungs.

You're not gonna die this way, Allen. No way, no how.

"Hey!" a familiar voice shouted. "Get off! He's mine!"

Barry managed to swivel just enough to see the owner of the voice: Eddie Thawne. The Eddie Thawne of Earth 27, to be exact. Unlike his Earth 1 counterpart—who'd nobly sacrificed his life to save the world from Reverse-Flash—this version was petty, venal, and thoroughly evil. He was also, unfortunately, a speedster with the name Johnny Quick. During his time on Earth 27, Barry had defeated Quick and liberated that version of Central City from his despotic reign. Someone must have broken him out of the special cell he'd been put in, just in time to let him run through the breach and into Barry's nightmares.

Thawne sped over to Barry's side and grabbed him by the shoulders. "Thought you were gonna leave me in that stupid prison you made, did you? Thought you could *win?*" He kneed Barry in the gut and laughed when Barry sank to his knees; the lasso had just barely enough slack to allow it. "You thought you could beat me? I'm Johnny Quick! I always win! Not so smart now, huh? Got nothing to say, slowpoke?"

"Busy . . . dying . . ." Barry managed to croak out, still trying to pull the lasso away from his throat so that he could recapture some precious air.

Johnny Quick's eyes narrowed. As though seeing it for the very first time, he stared at the shining, glowing, golden noose around Barry's neck, then followed it with his eyes back to Superwoman, who stood about ten feet away.

"Hey!" he shouted. "Lay off, Superwoman! I want this one!"

"Possession is ten-tenths of the law!" she snapped back. "Go get your own toy."

"I want *this* one!" Johnny Quick growled and took off like a rocket. In half a blink, he was at Superwoman's side, grabbing her wrists and trying to wrench the lasso out of her grip.

"Slow-witted buffoon!" she shouted.

"Treacherous harpy!" he shouted back.

As they struggled over the lasso, it loosened the tiniest bit on Barry's end. He could breathe just a bit . . .

. . . and then the two villains grappled with each other and took off, half flying, half running, dragging Barry behind them.

Oh, this is gonna suck . . . he predicted.

Bam! He slammed into a parked car. *Smack!* Right into a mailbox. *Crash!* "Sorry!" Colliding with a cluster of panicked evacuees.

Superwoman and Johnny Quick traded blows and insults as they blazed a trail up Kanigher Avenue, then veered to the right and smashed through the heavy glass doors of a nearby building. Superwoman seemed impervious to the shattered glass, and Johnny Quick vibrated through it. Barry, still unable to vibrate, got hit with dozens of shards of flying glass. Most of it was deflected by his costume, but he did take a few cuts across his exposed face and one just above his eye.

One centimeter lower and they'd call me One-Eye, he thought mordantly as blood dripped into his field of vision. He was being dragged through the lobby of the building, smashing back and forth against marble columns, his entire body battered and bruised. How much longer could he withstand this? How much longer could they go on? And what about the people out in the streets? Without him out there, there was no one to guide them to safety or protect them from Ultraman and Power Ring, who surely would stop fighting each other and turn their attentions groundward again soon.

All in all, it was shaping up to be a lousy showing for Central City's favorite hero.

C'mon, Barry. You can do this. You ran a thousand years into the future. Defeated a space pirate. Saved the sixty-fourth century from a clan of warring techno-wizards. Stop feeling sorry for yourself and make it happen!

He wrapped his legs around a nearby post and took the

lasso in both hands. It was time to pull instead of being pulled. Maybe while Superwoman was distracted by Johnny Quick, he could yank her end out of her hands . . .

Just then, there was a sudden ear-splitting screech that drowned out everything else. Barry gritted his teeth against it, but it stopped as abruptly as it had started.

"Sonics detected," a soothing voice said in Barry's ear. "Countermeasures deployed."

Thank God for Cisco Ramon, he thought. They'd faced enough enemies with sonic powers that Cisco had built a gadget into his suit that detected metahuman sonic frequencies and used a digital signal processor to broadcast an inverse opposing frequency to cancel it out. He was momentarily deaf, but at least his hearing was protected.

A lasso length away, Superwoman clapped her hands to her ears, dropping her end of the rope. Johnny Quick dropped to the floor, protecting his ears, too, clearly screaming in pain.

There, in the wrecked doorway of the building lobby, stood the greatest sight for sore eyes Barry had ever seen, a slender woman with a flowing mane of gold-highlighted hair and a sleek black costume with matching black domino mask: Black Canary.

"I have never been so glad to see you," Barry said. "Or hear you."

Dinah Drake had the power to generate and project high-frequency sonic waves with her throat. Clutching her signature bo staff weapon in one hand, she gave Barry a thumbs-up with the other but didn't smile or say hello— she was maintaining the frequencies, her assault rendering Superwoman and Johnny Quick temporarily helpless.

Barry pulled the lasso over his head. He was shaking, and not in the good way that meant he was vibrating through something. His whole body was oxygen starved; his adrenaline was sky-high. He needed a moment to recuperate.

But moments—especially for the Flash—were too precious to waste on recovery. The lasso still glowed in his hands, so he theorized that it had an innate power of its own, rather than merely projecting some sort of energy from Superwoman. On shaky legs, he made his way over to Superwoman and Johnny Quick, who were still on the floor, clutching their ears. Swiftly, he used the lasso to bind their wrists behind them.

Sound filled the lobby again as Black Canary took a deep breath. "Are they . . . ?"

He watched as the two villains struggled against the lasso and made absolutely no progress at all. "They're done for now," Barry announced. "Thanks, Canary. What took you guys so long?"

"Supersonic jet," she said. "What's wrong, speed of sound not fast enough for you?"

He grinned. "Not hardly." And then he bounced on his toes to test his legs and ran outside as fast as he could.

The breach had turned downtown Central City into a war zone, and things weren't getting any better. There were still people streaming out of the breach, though Barry could see that the flow had diminished some, and the crowd on the other side desperate to get through had shrunk quite a bit. He felt a spasm of relief, then a shiver of reproach. If people were in dire straits and needed to abandon Earth 27, he should be hoping for *more* evacuees, not fewer.

Overhead, Ultraman dipped low and fired a laser blast from his eyes. A furrow opened up in the middle of the street, scattering the fleeing crowd of hundreds as they tried to evade the sudden up-splash of molten asphalt.

"This guy and the one with the ring thing are giving us some trouble." It was Oliver, rushing over to stand next to Barry. His left cheek was scraped almost raw, the blood still wet and glimmering. He had dirt smudged over most of his face, and Barry saw that half his quiver was empty. Green Arrow had already fired a lot of his arsenal at the enemy.

"Tried explosive arrow, injection arrow, a nanite arrow . . ."

"What about the boxing glove arrow?" Barry asked.

"Smart-ass," Oliver deadpanned, watching as Ultraman executed a flip in midair. "He's coming back for another strafing run. This guy reminds me of that evil Supergirl from Earth X we fought last year."

Barry nodded. He'd thought the same thing. "Got a kryptonite arrow?"

"Yeah. But only one. I can't risk anything but a perfect shot."

"I thought you only took perfect shots, Ollie."

"Don't call me Ollie," Green Arrow growled, then leaped to one side as a chunk of concrete dropped from above. Barry vibrated into intangibility as the chunk smashed into the street and sprayed debris in all directions. Up in the sky, Power Ring had created a giant green claw and was using it to rip pieces out of buildings and hurl them below.

"This isn't going to go well," Barry said. "We need more muscle."

Oliver shook his head. "Spartan is trying to draw the ring guy away from innocents, and I've got Wild Dog and Mr. Terrific helping with crowd control. There's no one else."

Barry tapped his comms. "Wrong. Vibe, do you read me?"

Cisco Ramon winced as he breached from S.T.A.R. Labs to the rooftop of the Great Mark Hotel. He'd misjudged the height of the building by a tiny bit and landed hard on his left foot, twisting his ankle slightly. *This is not off to an auspicious start*, he thought.

He'd developed his vibe powers a couple of years ago, but they had, truthfully, frightened him a bit. He was a man of science and rationality, and while he understood how superpowers worked, the idea of bending the laws of physics in his bare hands was still a little . . . freaky.

So he'd forsaken those powers for a long time, not learning how to use them, especially the more offensively inclined powers, like the sonic vibe blasts he could shoot out of his hands. When absolutely necessary, he would open a breach somewhere or use his tactile clairvoyance to figure something out, as when he'd touched Madame Xanadu, but overall, he was happiest not as superhero Vibe but rather as Cisco Ramon, Mad Scientist–about-town.

Breaching from one universe to another was one thing. But for some reason—he hadn't quite worked it out yet— breaches *within* a universe were difficult and often painful.

But sometimes you just had to step up.

"I'm here," he said into his comms, ignoring the pain from his ankle. "Point me in the right direction."

From S.T.A.R. Labs, Iris crackled in his ear. "Satellite tracking shows this 'Power Ring' heading north over Novick, bearing six degrees."

Cisco spun around, oriented himself, and scanned the sky. "I got nothing. Your satellite is all fakakta."

"It's *your* satellite," she reminded him. "And I'm

watching his dot right now. He's practically on top of you. And since when do you speak Yiddish?"

Frustrated, Cisco turned again, craning his neck up, looking for the green blur of motion Barry had described to him. Nothing.

And then it hit him. *Duh! Idiot!*

He rushed to the edge of the building and peered over the parapet. For a sickening moment, the distance to the ground seemed to contract, the street rushing up to him, but then his equilibrium settled.

And there, a couple of stories *below* him, floating in the air like he just don't care . . . was Power Ring.

"I got him," Cisco told Iris. The villain was smashing windows and walls with a giant green fist that glowed with malevolent energy. The building shook beneath Cisco's feet, and debris rained down on the fleeing crowd.

Cisco licked his lips. Power Ring wasn't looking up; all his focus was on the building and the damage he could cause.

Don't mess this up. Don't mess this up.

"Hey, Cisco, any day now!"

Cisco almost jumped out of his skin. A tiny metallic sphere had drifted over to him, utterly silent. He recognized it—one of Mr. Terrific's T-spheres, a semiautonomous mobile computer.

"Buzz off, you *Phantasm* reject," Cisco snarled. "I was just about to save the day."

"We're getting crushed by the crowd down here, so whatever you're gonna do, do it fast!"

Cisco zapped the sphere with a stronger vibe blast than he'd intended. He'd meant to shove it away from him, and instead he sent it hurtling the length of the rooftop, where it spun around for a few seconds, then dropped over the edge and out of sight.

"Mr. Terrific," he muttered. "No self-esteem issues on Team Arrow."

Okay, Francisco. You can do this. You can totally *do this. It's only, like, thousands of lives and hundreds of millions of dollars in property damage on the line. So, you know, nothing to stress over.*

Licking his lips again, he cracked his neck left, then right. He leaned over the parapet again. Wiggled his fingers to loosen them up.

"Zippity-zappity," he muttered to himself. "How hard can it be?"

With a deep breath, he extended his arms out to their full length, aiming both hands at Power Ring. Inside, from some well of power that defied physics, he felt the vibrations beginning, an almost cold sensation in the pit of his stomach. It was like a sneeze, building and building, only instead of feeling it in his head, he felt it at his core. And instead of coming out his nose . . .

Vommmmmmmmmmmmm

The vibe blast radiated out from his hands, sonic frequencies rippling the air. Power Ring never saw it coming, and by the time he heard it . . . it was already there.

"Ba-*bam*!" Cisco chortled, fist-pumping triumphantly as Power Ring shouted out in alarm.

And dropped out of the sky.

"Whoops," Cisco said.

"Bar— Uh, Flash, this is Vibe. Look *up*!"

At the sound of Cisco's voice over the comms, Barry and Oliver, who had struggled through the crowd to an empty spot of pavement, looked up. In stark relief against the black backdrop of the night sky, a human figure plummeted through the air toward them.

"We should step aside," Oliver commented.

"He's gonna hit!" Barry warned.

"Let him."

"No!" Barry couldn't believe Oliver was serious.

"He's a bad guy," Oliver pointed out. "I don't want to kill him, but I don't have to save him."

Barry grimaced and took off. He ran up the side of the building, doing calculations in his head the whole time. Sure,

sure—it *looked* easy: You run up the side of the building and jump out to catch the guy who's falling. Piece of cake, right?

Nope. It was all physics and trigonometry. Everything had to be planned down to the microsecond. Push off from the building at the wrong time or at the wrong angle and you'll either miss the guy entirely or—maybe worse—end up colliding with him so forcefully that you might as well have let him smash into the ground.

Superspeed was an awesome power, but it involved a heck of a lot of homework.

Barry thought, *AONES*.

AONES. **A**t **O**r **N**ear **E**arth's **S**urface.

That was the relevant factor here. At or near Earth's surface, objects—or stunned super villains—accelerated at a reliably understandable rate of 9.8 meters per second squared. Power Ring had been close to the top of the building, which was about 120 meters high, as best Barry could tell. Figure Power Ring's mass to be about 80 kilograms. Barry knew the formula for calculating the velocity of a falling body: You simply took the square root of the quantity of the height of the building times two, times the AONES constant of 9.8. So, when Power Ring hit the ground, he would do so at 48.5 meters per second. Which was almost the same as being hit by a car going 70 miles an hour.

In other words, Power Ring would be paste.

Fortunately, it took almost five whole seconds to fall that far, which was longer than Barry actually needed.

Power Ring was already halfway to the ground, just beginning to shake off the effects of Cisco's blast. The green ring on his right fist was sputtering and spitting little verdant sparks in all directions, almost as though it were a flooded car engine that just couldn't catch.

Barry calculated the angle he needed, factored in Power Ring's direction and velocity, and realized that he needed to jump . . .

NOW!

He shoved off from the building. Lightning crackled around him. The air smelled of ozone. He reached out with both arms.

Power Ring dropped right into Barry's grasp. Barry tightened his arms around the villain. "Got you!"

Let's hear it for math homework. And they used to laugh at me for actually studying during study hall . . .

Power Ring gibbered unintelligibly. They were still falling.

I hope Oliver has figured out the obvious by now . . .

Barry churned his legs in the air, creating an enormous amount of friction, as well as a windy updraft. The combination slowed them down, but not so much that they wouldn't be pulped on landing.

Just then, he risked a glance below and saw Green

Arrow, off to one side, standing perfectly still as hordes of frightened citizens flowed around him. Oliver was like a rock jutting out of a river, immobile, focused, his bow drawn, an arrow aimed.

Yes! Do it, Oliver!

Green Arrow loosed the arrow. It soared into the empty space just below the falling duo, then split apart. Strong cables shot off in all directions, and suddenly there was a stout net, anchored at four points on the building, a lamppost, and a nearby billboard advertising the Central City Diamonds baseball team.

Barry and Power Ring crashed into the net, which held . . .

. . . for about three seconds before breaking . . .

. . . and spilling them into the air again.

But it had done its job—it broke their fall just enough, slowing their momentum, so that when they fell the last ten feet, it merely *hurt*.

Power Ring groaned and raised his fist. The green ring finally caught, and a wicked-looking mace appeared in the air.

Before Power Ring could do anything with it, though, Green Arrow crouched down and punched him once in the face. Hard. Power Ring slumped unconscious, collapsing on top of Barry, who'd borne the brunt of the impact.

"The only thing that doesn't hurt on me right now," Barry moaned, "is my eyelashes."

He took a moment to twist around and remove the ring from the villain's finger. It felt warm, pulsating gently in his hand. He shivered. It seemed completely harmless, but he sensed something malign and ill-intentioned about its power. Like a bad whisper in a dark room. He tucked it into a pocket.

"I knew you wouldn't let him die," Barry told Oliver.

"I was mostly trying to save *you*," Oliver said, helping Barry to his feet. "That's three down. And the worst one yet to go." He pointed up, where Ultraman had begun ripping big air condensers off rooftops and dropping them on the fleeing crowd. Black Canary and Mr. Terrific were doing a decent job deflecting the pieces, but it was exhausting, and they couldn't last forever.

"Time to bust out that kryptonite arrow," Barry said. "Let's go line up a perfect shot."

"Hey, everyone." Flash's voice came through the comms channel to everyone on-site from Teams Flash and Arrow. "We need to draw Ultraman into Green Arrow's line of sight, OK?"

"Ultraman?" It was Wild Dog. "Is that the name of the guy shooting fire out of his eyes up there?"

Sure enough, Ultraman was melting a mirrored wall on a skyscraper into a molten river that threatened to engulf some innocents below.

"Try to keep up, Wild Dog," Mr. Terrific said as the Flash moved the potential mirror victims out of harm's way.

"Cut the chatter," Green Arrow growled, "and divert that guy off the main avenue and into the street that cuts in from the northwest."

"Roger that," said Wild Dog.

"Copy," said Black Canary.

"Let's do this," Vibe chimed in.

7

REEN ARROW WAS POISED ON A ledge on a low building at the point where Novick Street met Guice Avenue in a T-intersection. From here, he could see the entire length of Novick, all the way to the park. He had a perfect vantage point. Now all he needed was a target.

He nocked the kryptonite arrow. It looked like any other arrow, with a long, straight shaft, custom fletching, and a tapered steel head. But that steel was an illusion. It was a thin layer of painted aluminum that concealed the glowing, green kryptonite beneath. It had cost Oliver a fortune to synthesize the element, based on astronomical observations of the radio spectrum of the planet Krypton in a far-off galaxy. It had been worth it last year when he'd faced down the evil Supergirl from Earth-X, and it would be doubly worth it now.

"I'm in position," he whispered into his comms.

"Copy," Flash responded. "Let's razzle-dazzle, everyone."

Cisco ran across the rooftop and closed his eyes as he jumped over the edge. The Great Mark Hotel was five hundred feet high. He had something like six seconds before impact, plenty of time to conjure a breach, even if it took him a couple of tries.

He nailed it in one. A breach opened up beneath him, and he plummeted through.

On the ground, Mr. Terrific watched as Ultraman swooped overhead. "C'mon, Vibe . . ." he mumbled under his breath. "Any day now . . ."

Before his eyes, the sky ripped open just above Ultraman. Cisco Ramon dropped out of nowhere and landed right on Ultraman's back.

The villain was completely caught off guard. He lurched in the air, trying to throw Cisco off, but Cisco had a good grip on Ultraman's cape.

"Now!" Mr. Terrific yelled. He sent a flurry of T-spheres into the sky, swarming Ultraman like flies on a sun-spoiled carcass.

The T-spheres spun and whirled around the villain, flashing strobe lights and emitting high-pitched squeals at random intervals. With a snarl, Ultraman batted some of them away and vaporized others with blasts of heat vision. Meanwhile, Cisco rode him like a bucking bronco at the world's worst, most dangerous rodeo.

"Canary! It's you!" Flash called out over their earpieces.

Black Canary was poised atop a nearby building. She took a deep breath and screamed out her Canary Cry so fiercely that it tore at her throat. Cisco bailed, zapping Ultraman with a vibe as he released the cape and dropped out of the sky again, falling into another breach just before a sizzling ray of heat vision could hit him.

Between the vibe blast, the T-spheres, and the Canary Cry, Ultraman was disoriented, his rage building.

And anger would make him sloppy, Barry knew. It was time.

The Flash ran up a building, leaped, and bounced off another one, gaining altitude and momentum, then pushed off one more time. He was on an arc path that would lead to a collision with Ultraman, moving at incredible superspeed.

The villain had destroyed the last of the T-spheres. He puckered his lips and blew a hurricane-like wind at the rooftop on which Black Canary stood. She tumbled over, grabbed a ventilation duct, and hung on for dear life.

Barry closed his eyes and tucked into a ball, then vibrated as he neared Ultraman, hoping that Kryptonian molecular structure wasn't *too* much denser than ordinary matter. Otherwise, this was going to hurt. A lot.

He vibrated straight through Ultraman. Whew! He hadn't been sure that was going to work—until it did.

Ultraman actually froze for a moment, hanging suspended in the air like an ornament without a tree. He stared, tracking Barry with his eyes as the Flash tumbled through him and past him, then landed on a nearby balcony and ran down the side of the building.

"What *are* you?" Ultraman demanded, and flew after him.

Barry pushed himself even faster. His whole body was one big bruise, but he couldn't give up now. He hit the street, turned left, and kept running. Ultraman tailed him, zipping down from above and cruising twenty feet or so off the ground, fists held out before him. Barry heard the crackle and pop of heat vision behind him; he darted left. A fire hydrant overheated and exploded, showering him with water and filling the air with steam. He fought to keep his footing on the suddenly slick road.

He raced down the street, keenly aware that he was only outpacing Ultraman by a few feet. Tossing glances over his shoulder, he juked left and right to avoid the sporadic blasts of heat vision. Sweat poured down his forehead, wicking into his eyes.

He cut a sharp left turn onto Novick Street.

Oliver watched as the Flash came around the corner and barreled down Novick toward him. He only had a split second—Barry was moving so fast that he was just a red blur and a yellowish coruscating cascade of lightning.

Right behind him was Ultraman. Barry put on a burst of speed and pulled ahead.

Oliver drew in a deep breath, then blew it out slowly. Archers never held their breath—the strain of holding all that air in the lungs could cause tiny muscle spasms, little vibrating shakes that could throw off the aim. He emptied his lungs, and when his body was completely at rest, he loosed the arrow.

With his speed-attuned senses, Barry watched the arrow as it left Oliver's sniper's nest. If the plan was working, Ultraman would be too distracted by his rage and his desire to kill Barry to notice something like an arrow.

The arrow sailed through the air, rising and then dipping ever so slightly with the motion of the air currents.

It's gonna miss, Barry thought.

No, wait, it's gonna hit.

He changed his mind ten times in a second, then stopped thinking about it. He had to trust that Oliver Queen, the greatest archer in the world, had compensated correctly for windage.

The arrow looked perfectly normal. And in fact, Ultraman spied it when it was halfway to him. He assessed it instantly and realized it couldn't hurt him. Pathetic. If the people on this Earth thought they could hurt him with an *arrow* . . . They might as well throw sticks and stones. Idiots.

So he ignored it, just as he ignored things like bullets, tank shells, surface-to-air missiles, and basic morality. All he cared about right now was getting his hands on this punk who thought he was Johnny Quick, breaking his stupid speedster legs in half, then ripping off the stumps. See how fast he could run then! Ha!

The arrow shuddered briefly and the aluminum shell split off, revealing the glowing kryptonite core. By now, it was less than two feet away from Ultraman, who was flying toward it at several times the speed of sound.

Barry spun around, running backward, grinning as the arrow and Ultraman ran into each other. A green puff marked the blast spot, and Ultraman pulled up short in the air, snatching the arrow by its shaft, snapping it in two instantly. The glowing green impact point of the arrow throbbed against his neck, pulsating like a heart-beat. Any second now, Barry knew from experience, Ultraman would drop from the sky like a clay pigeon at the Olympics.

The villain hovered for a moment, staring at the crushed arrow in his hand. He put one hand to his neck, where the kryptonite had hit him.

And then he laughed.

It wasn't an amused laugh; it was the angriest, most outraged laugh Barry had ever heard. It echoed in the concrete-and-glass canyon of Novick Street, shaking the windows until they shattered and rained glass down onto the abandoned sidewalks.

Ultraman threw down the arrow and inhaled mightily, puffing out his chest. His muscles—already enormous—seemed to swell, and his eyes glowed a sick and harsh red that was almost black.

Barry's mouth went dry and his heart hammered just a little too hard in his chest.

"Uh, guys?" Barry put out over the comms connection. He swallowed hard and paused. He couldn't believe what he was about to say. "We may have a little problem. Seems like kryptonite makes this guy *stronger*."

8

HE SHOULD HAVE REALIZED. Everything on Earth 27 was the opposite of the same thing on Earth 1. Good guys were bad, the Rogues were noble . . . so of course kryptonite wouldn't stop Ultraman.

"Oh, come on!" Cisco complained. "For real?"

"No one could have anticipated this!" Oliver protested. A ferocious blast of heat vision hit the building just below where he was standing, and his ledge exploded into fiery chunks of concrete and brick. He did a backflip, just barely avoiding being hit, the heels of his boots slightly singed as he careened into the window behind him. Fortunately, it was open. He lay sprawled out on the floor for a moment. It was someone's office. Empty, of course. Everyone had evacuated.

Another blast of heat vision. He clung to the floor. Fire suppression systems came online, sprinklers detecting the massive heat of Ultraman's attack. It was raining inside.

He scrambled to his feet and raced out into the hallway, then crashed through the emergency stairwell door and hopped over the banister, using a rope arrow to slide down three stories to the ground floor. Soon, he was out on the street, where Barry was running in a weaving zigzag pattern to avoid falling debris. Ultraman was eighty feet straight up, fists clenched, body engorged with power. He spun in a circle, devastating the buildings around him with a combination of ultra-breath and heat vision. Oliver had gone from raining water inside to raining buildings outside.

"You thought you could hurt me?" Ultraman screamed from above. "I'm a *god*, you little pukes! I'm indestructible! I am king of this world!" Ultraman roared. "I'm king of all worlds! You'll all bow down before me!"

He seemed to remember then that there were people he wanted to kill. He stopped spinning and scanned the ground, picking out Oliver and Barry among the piles of debris and the smoke purling up from the charred remains of buildings.

"You'll be first to die!" he howled, and launched himself at them, fists extended.

Before either of them could react, he vanished into a breach.

Cisco jogged around the corner, out of breath. "That . . ." he heaved, "was not . . . easy . . ."

"Where'd you send him?" Barry asked.

"Ten thousand miles thataway." Cisco pointed straight up. "Not that it matters. He'll be back any second."

"He's almost as fast as I am," Barry said. "And a lot stronger."

"And he shoots lasers out of his eyes," Oliver added.

"That part sort of sucks," Barry admitted.

"Guys," Mr. Terrific said into their earpieces, "I think I have a solution."

"We're all ears!" Cisco yelled.

"Flash, you need to do your vibrating trick again, only this time solidify for half a second when you're inside him. You'll cause a complete molecular disruption of his physical being."

Barry hesitated and looked over at Oliver, who had arched an approving eyebrow.

"I'd rather not kill him," Barry said.

"*I'd* rather not die," Oliver put in.

"You make a good point," Black Canary chimed in. "I'm voting with Green Arrow on this one."

"So, kryptonite doesn't work," Barry mused, thinking.

"Understatement!" Cisco yelled.

"On Earth 27, he had to cut a deal to share power with

the rest of the Crime Syndicate," Barry went on. "So he's not all-powerful. He's got to have a weakness."

"Or maybe no one on Earth 27 ever exposed him to the stuff that makes him stronger!" Cisco remonstrated.

"We couldn't know that!" Oliver shouted.

"Guys." Barry stood between them and held out both hands to calm them down. "We need to think this through."

"There's nothing to think about," Oliver said. "This is do-or-die, Barry. He can kill everyone on the planet."

A wind began to howl, funneling down from above. Ultraman was coming. There was no time.

No time for anyone else, at least. For the Flash, there was *always* time, and Barry used that time to think.

"What arrows do you have left?" he asked Oliver.

Oliver reached back and quickly ran his fingers over the Braille dots on the end of each arrow, reading the code that told him what each arrow did. "Nothing that'll stop him. Recording arrow. Fireworks. Zip tie. A bunch of normal arrows. Why?"

It would work, Barry figured. They just needed more time, that most precious of all commodities. "I'll distract him," he told Cisco and Oliver. "Meanwhile . . ." And he filled them in on his idea.

Cisco swallowed hard. "But what if his powers don't work the way other people's do? We'll be in the same position."

Barry hesitated. "Then we'll discuss Mr. Terrific's idea. But first we try this."

He cupped his hands and shouted up into the sky: "Hey, you lard-brained imbecile! If you want to be king of this world, you'll have to go through me first!"

Given how tired and bruised he was, the last thing Barry wanted was to run, but run he did, pushing himself to his limit. A blue-and-red streak broke free from the clouds, and with an enraged roar, Ultraman surged through the air, his eyes spitting pure lava in every direction.

Barry led him on a merry chase through Central City, trying to keep his turns tight and his race route confined to the areas of the city that had already been damaged in the melee. No sense destroying more property, right?

They raced past the breach, now devoid of evacuees. Except for a few stragglers making their slow way uptown, the area was empty and eerily quiet save for a low hum coming from the breach. The air had gone even more foul, reeking of abandoned houses and old, stale grass clippings. He now had a clearer line of sight to the figure within. It was truly massive, a mile distant, walking at a slow, implacable pace that said it was in no particular hurry, that in the end it would win, that—

Barry was almost caught out by Ultraman, swooping low to the ground, reaching out with grasping, too-strong hands. He goosed his speed and dodged, slipped left, then ran up Schwartz Street, doubling back toward Novick.

It was hard to hit that sweet spot of letting Ultraman chase him but not catch him, but he managed, slowing down just enough to let the villain stay close, then putting on a burst of speed when those hands neared him, or when the heat of those laser eyes made sweat bubble at the base of his neck.

They needed Ultraman focused entirely on *him*, not on anything else. He assumed Ultraman had Supergirl's senses, too—it was tough to fool someone who could hear your every whisper, look through your body at a glance to see what was behind your back, examine you down to the genes. But Barry had been right—everyone had a weakness, and Ultraman's rage was his. He was so determined to kill the Flash that he wasn't paying attention to anyone else.

"We're ready," Oliver's voice whispered in Barry's ear.

Finally! It had felt like forever, but he and Ultraman had been dancing their unique waltz for only thirty seconds, albeit at superspeed.

He slowed down just a bit. Not enough to make it look deliberate, but just enough that Ultraman would think he'd actually caught up. The next thing Barry knew, those incredibly strong hands were on his body, grinding the bones in his shoulders together. He yelped in pain, not faking it at all. If the others didn't come through, he'd be the Fastest Paste Alive in mere seconds.

Ba-boom! Whiiiiiiish! Ka-pop!

A series of mini-explosions off to their left, concomitant with eruptions of color. Blues, reds, purples, and yellows flowered into the evening air. Ultraman grunted in surprise and glanced left to see . . .

Cisco, standing on the sidewalk near a bus stop, holding Oliver's fireworks arrow up and away from his body, wincing as each firework went off.

Peeee-yow! A blazing trail of red-and-green sparks ended in an explosive spiderweb of color.

Barry lurched forward and vibrated out of Ultraman's clutches. The villain was fast and strong and invulnerable. Given half a second, he could easily avoid the next arrow Oliver fired at him.

But Oliver had fired the arrow two seconds ago while Ultraman was distracted by the fireworks. It was already passing through Barry's intangible form. Not even Ultraman could evade it.

The zip-tie arrow spun on its axis and expanded into something that was very definitely *not* a zip tie. Two metallic rings clamped around Ultraman's wrists, connected by a short cylinder that glowed blue.

Ultraman growled with annoyance and flexed his considerable muscles. Nothing happened.

He grunted and leaned toward Cisco, thrusting out his nose as though he expected something to happen. It was the same expression he had when using his heat vision—but nothing happened.

"What did you do?" he screamed, his voice laden with anger. "What did you do to me?" He struggled against the handcuffs, tugging, pulling, straining. Veins stood out at his temples and along the sides of his neck, but nothing could budge those manacles.

"We modified the zip-tie arrow to use S.T.A.R. Labs' anti-metahuman shackles," Cisco told him with a satisfied grin. "I invented them. That lovely feeling of powerlessness and vulnerability you're experiencing? You're welcome."

"I'll kill every last one of you!" Ultraman raged, swinging his arms around, straining against the cuffs. "I'll murder every living thing on this planet, then burn it to a crisp from outer space!"

Cisco put a hand over his heart. "Heavens me! You're a naughty boy, aren't you?"

Ultraman screamed an inarticulate, wordless scream, stomping his feet, gnashing his teeth. "You'll all die! Every one of you! I swear it!"

Nearby, Barry was bent over, hands on knees, panting, trying to reoxygenate his cells. "Could someone . . . shut this guy . . . up?" he managed.

Oliver stepped over, wound up his right arm, and punched Ultraman in the jaw. The villain uttered a sound like *Flurk!* and collapsed in an unconscious heap.

Mr. Terrific and Black Canary came running around the corner and beheld Ultraman crumpled on the ground.

"What took you guys so long?" Cisco asked.

Mr. Terrific held up a T-sphere. "I was modifying one of these babies to mimic solar radiation in the red portion of the color spectrum. To turn off his powers."

"Too late," Cisco said. "But nice try."

At S.T.A.R. Labs, they were at capacity. Iris was coordinating . . . well, *everything*, from the main board in the Cortex.

In the medical bay, Caitlin was patching up Wild Dog, who'd been hit with shrapnel during the battle. Everyone else had injuries, too, but they would have to wait.

"Take a number and form an orderly line," Caitlin told them. "I'll get to you when I get to you."

Barry had managed to catch his breath again, and his entire body ached like he'd skied down Everest, but he was confident that his accelerated metabolism would fix most of what ailed him. He left the others in the infirmary and ambled out into the Cortex. Iris was rotating back and forth from monitor to monitor.

"What can I help with?" Barry asked, sidling up to her.

She hip-checked him out of her way and turned to another keyboard. "Sorry, babe, but I've got a system here. Hey, FDCC, this is S.T.A.R. Labs. Are those pyronullifiers we sent along holding up?"

Over the communications link, a voice crackled back to her: "Hey, S.T.A.R. Labs, this is FDCC Ladder Company Number 52. These things are *awesome*! We've got a five-alarmer under control and will be moving on to the fire at Bates and Schwartz in a few minutes."

"Great!" Iris told him. "Let me know if we can help out in any other way." She broke the connection and offered Barry a quick, genuine smile. "I've got it under control. I just need to do it my way, you know?"

Barry took in the screens. Iris was coordinating all sorts of interagency responses to the breach—police, fire, ambulance . . . The FBI and A.R.G.U.S. were both on the scene as well. One camera showed a group of people filing into what looked like the baseball stadium. Fortunately, the Diamonds were playing an away series, so the place was empty.

"I'm putting the speedsters from Earth 27 there," she told him. "Just temporarily, until we can figure out where to put them permanently." She shrugged. "I can't think of a safe place for that many people who can move at super-speed. I thought Johnny Quick's formula didn't work on Earth 1?"

Earth 27's corrupt Eddie Thawne had become the evil speedster Johnny Quick by reciting a special formula—3X2(9YZ)4A—that focused his mind and allowed him to tap into the Speed Force (or, as Eddie called it, HyperHeaven). Upon returning from Earth 27, Barry had tried the formula . . . and realized it did nothing for him on Earth 1. But now there were Earth 27 refugees zipping around Central City like nobody's business. To say nothing of Johnny Quick himself.

"I guess it *does* work here after all," Barry told her. "But there must be an upper limit and I'm already above it."

"So," she mused, "they'll never be as fast as you, as long as they're here on Earth 1. That's something, at least."

Barry sighed and peered up at the main monitor. Feeding into it was a camera view from a rig CCPD had set up near the breach. The area was completely evacuated now—the locals dispersed to shelters, the speedster refugees gathering at the stadium. The breach sizzled and crackled with a burnt-orange light at its ragged edges, and the walking figure seemed closer to Earth 1.

"We have to figure this out," Barry said. From his own pocket, he withdrew the ring that Power Ring had worn. "Maybe this thing can help." He bounced it up and down in his palm. "If we can figure out how it works."

Cisco breezed by and snatched it out of the air mid-bounce. "You've come to the right place, my friend. S.T.A.R. Labs: We hack reality so you don't have to."

"How's our patient?" Barry asked as Caitlin hustled past him carrying a roll of gauze and pair of medical scissors.

"Sleeping, last I checked," she said over her shoulder. "I'll look in on her in a minute."

Barry shrugged and called up the camera from the medical bay on the next level down, where Madame Xanadu was resting, just to see for himself. He gasped. Iris, nearby, glanced at the same monitor and did a double take.

The camera showed someone in her room!

Iris's jaw dropped. "No alarms went off! How did he get in here?"

Barry was already gone, grabbing Cisco by the arm to drag him to the stairs, then down to the floor below and into the medical bay.

Sure enough, a man stood at Madame Xanadu's bed,

bent over as though to kiss her. But she was no Sleeping Beauty and he was no Prince Charming. He wore a deep blue suit and jacket, with a matching fedora and a white turtleneck. His clothing was immaculate, save for his shoes, which were dirty, scuffed, and worn as though he'd walked every inch of the universe to arrive at this place and time.

"Step away from her!" Barry ordered, and when the man straightened up, Barry gaped in recognition.

The shadow cast by the brim of the man's hat hid his eyes, but the pendant around his neck and the set of his jaw were unmistakable. "I saw you on Earth 27," Barry said, shocked.

"You know this guy?" Cisco said in surprise. "What's he doing here?"

"I don't really *know* him. He was in Madame Xanadu's shop on the other Earth. He's her friend."

"Not a friend," the man said, shaking his head. "A mere stranger, though known to many, Barry Allen. Perhaps even known by you, in the future."

The future . . . Barry suddenly thought of Citizen Hefa, the Quantum Police officer from the sixty-fourth century who'd helped him track down Abra Kadabra. She had said at one point that that visit was his *first* trip to the future. Was there going to be a second?

After being lost for a moment in the very idea, he

snapped himself out of the possible future and back to the very definite present. "How did you get to Earth 1?" he asked the stranger.

"Duh," Cisco said. "He came through the breach, like everyone else. The big question is: *Why* are you here?"

The stranger sniffed as though offended but too enlightened to say so. "Gashes in the very fabric of the soul of reality are of no use to me. I travel by my own lights." He gestured to Madame Xanadu. "Her spirit weakens. Her pain is great, cut off so suddenly from her doppelgänger."

"Tell us something we don't know," Cisco snarked.

The stranger's lips quirked into something that was almost a smile. "There are many such things I could tell you. For now, I will satisfy myself to tell you what you face."

"The creature in the breach." Barry's spine stiffened.

"Yes. It is called Anti-Matter Man. It comes from outside the Multiverse as you know it."

"I'm getting a little tired of *that*," Cisco muttered.

"You know of the fifty-three universes of the Multiverse," the stranger said. And that was true enough— so far as they knew, there were fifty-two parallel universes, plus the universe inhabited by Earth-X, for a total of fifty-three. "But there is another aspect to the Multiverse. All the universes you have encountered are composed of positive matter. There is another universe, an *antiverse*, made of anti-matter. It is from this universe that Anti-Matter Man hails."

Anti-matter. It was just like regular matter, except the particles were diametrically opposite. In positive matter, atoms were made up of a neutral or positively charged nucleus surrounded by negatively charged electrons. In anti-matter, the nucleus was neutral or *negatively* charged, surrounded by positively charged positrons.

Matter and anti-matter were completely harmless . . . until they met. When they touched . . .

"Boom," Barry whispered. As a being composed of anti-matter, Anti-Matter Man's mere presence was wreaking havoc on the positive matter world of Earth 27, breaking down the laws of physics and causing mass devastation.

"There is no planet Earth in the antiverse," the stranger went on, "but there is a world called Qward. Qward is a place of pure malevolence, and Anti-Matter Man is a walking, living expression of that evil. He is more than a hundred meters tall, and beyond the considerable powers he possesses, in a positive matter universe his mere touch brings explosive decay and death. The Weaponers of Qward created Anti-Matter Man as a weapon, to be used in an invasion of the positive matter universes. But so great and terrible was his power that even the Weaponers feared him.

And so they locked away their creation, sealing him within the core of a moon."

"How did he get out?" Barry asked.

"More important than such trifling facts," the stranger remonstrated, "is that he *is* out. And as Anti-Matter Man walks through the positive matter universes, he corrodes, corrupts, and destroys them. The world you designate Earth 27 is already corrupted beyond habitation. Its atmosphere is toxic, its biosphere disintegrating."

Barry and Cisco shared a worried glance. "And I thought evil super-Nazis from Earth-X were a problem," Cisco said. "This guy could actually destroy the universe."

"How do we stop it?" Barry asked, then did a double take, grabbing Cisco's elbow and pointing.

Madame Xanadu lay peacefully asleep in her bed. The stranger, though, was gone.

9

N STAR CITY, FELICITY SMOAK STARED at her computer screen. Then, with a quiet moan of frustration, she lightly rapped her forehead against her desk.

"We are the stupidest smart people in the world," she said aloud to no one. She was alone in the Bunker, but she went ahead and said it out loud again, just to hear the words, the harsh truth.

She'd completely disassembled the explosive device the Flash had recovered, examining and analyzing not just each component but also how they fit together. That gave her a bomber's profile, something she could run against databases from Interpol, A.R.G.U.S., the FBI, and more. Building a bomb was delicate, dangerous work—bombers liked to find a method that worked for them and stick with it. So it was possible to track bombers by their tendencies, the same way police used a criminal's modus operandi to track him or her down.

That part of her investigation was going really, really well. She had a 99.87 percent database match to a bomber named Irwin Schwab, who often went by the code name Ambush. In a series of bombings throughout Asia and parts of Africa, Ambush had used explosive devices nearly identical to the one the Flash had recovered, each time avoiding casualties but still causing massive property loss. She felt pretty certain she'd identified the bomber.

But she'd missed something else. All of them had.

There had been three successful bombings. And it turned out that each of those bombings corresponded to a break-in at a very high-tech facility. The Star City locations for Palmer Technologies, Kord Omniversal Research and Development, and Mercury Labs had all been burgled at the same time as the three successful bombings. Nothing had been taken at any of the would-be robberies, though.

But this very night, during what was supposed to be the *fourth* bombing . . .

"ALL UNITS ALERT!" read the encrypted email she'd intercepted from A.R.G.U.S. "Star City facility on lockdown! DO NOT APPROACH! No personnel in or out!"

Ambush had been using the bombings as a distraction while he made his way inside some of the most secure tech facilities in the world, looking for something.

Something that he'd found at A.R.G.U.S. That encrypted message, that lockdown . . . All that meant more than a simple breach of security. They were in lockdown because they had to figure out what was missing and how to get it back.

She'd sent a message offering help to Lyla Michaels, the director of A.R.G.U.S. and, conveniently enough, Diggle's wife. The message had bounced off A.R.G.U.S.'s cyber-shielding. Until they figured out what was missing, they weren't going to let any data in or out, either.

So Ambush was looking for something. He was willing to knock down buildings to get it. And now, whatever it is, he has it.

She ran her fingers over the communications switches. She'd taken things as far as she could on her own. No matter what was happening in Central City, she needed to get Oliver back.

10

AT S.T.A.R. LABS, BARRY STOOD in the Pipeline with Cisco and Oliver.

Originally, the Pipeline had served as a series of holding cells for the various super villains the Flash defeated in and around Central City. But after a while, the extralegal nature of the facility made Barry uncomfortable. He was essentially running an off-the-books prison, and that just didn't sit right with him from a human rights standpoint. Nowadays, metahumans who broke the law were incarcerated in a special wing of Iron Heights Penitentiary, their powers nullified by a series of overlapping energy fields devised by Cisco, using the same tech they'd used in the Pipeline originally.

Still, occasionally there were bad guys who just didn't fit

into the legal system, and on those occasions, the Pipeline was ready. For, say, time travelers like Abra Kadabra.

Or, as now, villains from another universe.

The Crime Syndicate of America was locked up in four holding cells arrayed around a central node. From their position, Barry, Cisco, and Oliver could see into each of the four cells, but the villains couldn't see one another. Ultraman, Power Ring, Superwoman, and Johnny Quick were powerless and helpless.

"Where's the fifth member of your little club of evil?" Barry asked, remembering his time on Earth 27. "Where's Owlman?"

"Owlman?" Cisco blurted out. "What kind of name is that?"

"Could we focus on what matters?" Oliver asked.

"This *does* matter! Owlman? I mean . . . I guess I get it," Cisco admitted, contemplating. "Owls are predators. They operate at night. Super-quiet fliers. They're swift, talon-y death birds from the dark skies. As far as nocturnal critters go, it's not bad. I mean, if you want to be really silly, they could have gone with Bat—"

"Focus!" Oliver intoned, making Cisco jump a little.

"Owlman," Barry said again to the villains. "Where is he?"

They said nothing. "I ain't no snitch," Power Ring finally said with something resembling pride.

"How admirable of you," Oliver said in a voice dripping with insincerity. "Flash, give me five minutes alone with any of them, and I'll have answers for you."

Barry shrugged. He had never been great at playing Good Cop/Bad Cop. He preferred to reason with people, even villains. But the CSA came from a world where their evil was lauded, rewarded, and perpetuated. They might not respond to anything resembling logic.

Still, he had to try. "I won't have Owlman out on the streets of my city, causing problems," Barry told them. "Tell me where he went and how to find him, and we can consider better quarters for you four."

Superwoman laughed and slammed her palms against the reinforced thymoglass that separated her from the rest of the world and her powers. "Why should we be afraid of someone so weak and needy?" she asked. "If you really wanted to get us to cooperate, you'd've killed one of us by now to prove your strength."

Ugh. The twisted logic of Earth 27 was no help to him here.

"Fine," Oliver said, unslinging his bow. "Open up a cage, Flash. I'll pick one of them off before the door's all the way open."

"Whoa, whoa, whoa!" Cisco stepped between Oliver and the cells. "Maybe we try something different before we go putting arrows in people's eyes?"

Oliver hissed his anger and adjusted his aim over Cisco's shoulder. "Never—*ever*—come between me and a shot."

"Guys!" Barry took each of them by the wrist and pulled them apart. In the cells, Johnny Quick and Ultraman were laughing. Superwoman had turned away in disgust, and Power Ring was just sitting on the floor, making shadow puppets on the wall.

Out in the hallway, out of earshot of the Crime Syndicate, Barry released Cisco and Oliver, who took a step apart, sizing each other up.

"You were playing it too hard, man!" Cisco said.

"Who says I was playing?" Oliver asked. "I know how to make it look like I'm shooting to kill without actually killing."

Cisco barked laughter. "So, what, you take out an eye or put an arrow in someone's femoral artery to make a point?"

"To save lives?" Oliver spat back, his anger barely controlled. "Absolutely."

Barry came between them again. "Guys, we're not getting anywhere. I'm gonna—"

"Green Arrow, Green Arrow." It was Iris's voice coming over the facility-wide public address system. "I have a comm from the Bunker for you."

Oliver grunted and, with one final, withering look at Cisco, turned on his heel and marched off.

"That guy is too hard-core," Cisco complained when he and Barry were alone.

"Don't be too hard on him. He's had a rough time, rougher than we have. His outlook is a little dark, but his heart's in the right place."

Cisco sighed and rubbed his eyes, yawning. "It's been a day and a half, crammed into one day," he said. "What are we going to do about Owlman? And Anti-Matter Man, for that . . . matter." He winced. "Didn't mean that pun. I am *so* much better than that. You know, right?"

"I do," Barry reassured him, clapping him on the shoulder. "Let's go see what Felicity has, and then we'll figure out where to go from there."

11

LYLA MICHAELS PRESSED HER palms against her eyes, blotting out the world. It was easier this way. Easier when she couldn't see the world, when it all just went away.

A.R.G.U.S. Advanced Research Group United Support. One of the most secretive and powerful organizations in the country. All hers. Being director of A.R.G.U.S. had been a dream fulfilled, but the funny thing about dreams was this: All you had to do was turn the wrong corner in your dreamworld, and you'd find yourself in a nightmare.

She had responsibilities that most people could not fathom. Under her watch was an organization devoted to wrangling the uncontrollable, comprehending the impenetrable, and deflecting the unstoppable. She'd dealt with time travelers, mystics, aliens, mad scientists, and just plain lunatics. And that was just on the weekends.

Her husband, John Diggle, had told her that there was a serial bomber in the city but that she needn't worry about it, because Green Arrow was on the case. And she had gratefully allowed her mind not to wander in that direction, focusing instead on the hard work of A.R.G.U.S.

But now there seemed to be a connection. She had a readout on her desk that told her someone had broken into an A.R.G.U.S. lab that very night, stealing something very dangerous.

No one was supposed to know where that lab was. No one was supposed to know that the lab even existed in the first place.

And yet . . .

With a heavy, reluctant sigh, she pulled her hands away from her face. Light danced into her eyes, her vision clearing. She ran a hand through her short hair. Right at this moment, she wanted nothing more than to go home, tell the babysitter to take the rest of the night off, and cuddle her daughter, Sara. Hold her close and safe.

But she had a job to do. She didn't get to shirk her duty just because it was tough sometimes.

She tapped one immaculately manicured finger on the sheet of paper on her desk. It was titled "INCIDENT

REPORT: MISSING ITEMS." What followed was a lot of jargon and technical mumbo jumbo, but only three words actually mattered.

Those three words were *Bug-Eyed Bandit*.

There is a part of Star City where the tourists never go, unless they get lost, take a wrong turn at Grell Park, and wind up ambling down a dark alley, turning left, then walking up a decrepit block of crumbling brownstones and broken macadam.

The only people who live here are the forgotten. The forsaken. The ones Star City would rather pretend don't exist. Some of them are here because they made mistakes. Some because they made bad choices. Some because they just had bad luck.

And one of them was here because it was exactly where he wanted to be.

In a dimly lit room in an old town house, the man some called Ambush sat at a desk. The desk had been retrieved from a garbage dumpster. It was made of steel, one leg dinged and bent, the surface pitted and scarred. There was a single lamp burning, an old clip-on sort, attached to the desktop, aimed precisely so that it formed an almost-perfect, sharp circle of white light on the desk's surface.

Ambush sat at the desk in a green T-shirt, his chair a similar dumpster-dive treasure, one wheel frozen in place. He wore a set of magnifying goggles, and with a pair of tweezers, he probed at the thing before him, the thing pinned down in that circle of white light.

It was a bug.

A tiny, mechanical insect. Such a faithful reproduction of real life that anyone looking at it would have thought it to be real. But it wasn't made of flesh and keratin and blood. It was manufactured out of bits of alloy and plastic and woven metallic fibers. It was a wondrous thing, a clone of nature, a perfection of the imperfect.

Ambush probed at its innards. He liked what he saw. He grinned broadly. "Oh, yes. This will be . . . advantageous."

12

THE CORTEX HUMMED WITH activity. Caitlin was following John Diggle around with a thermometer and a blood pressure cuff, but he was ignoring her, barking orders into a cell phone that he held in one hand while pressing a swatch of bloody gauze to a cut on his forehead with the other.

At the same time, Iris was giving commands to Mr. Terrific and Black Canary, who were hustling to control boards and relaying her instructions to those in the field. Central City recognized that when it came to metahumans and the problems they incurred, mere humans could not prevail. At times like this, the city had a contract with S.T.A.R. Labs to help coordinate responses, and now Iris was basically running the show. She was helping Mercury Labs scientists take readings from the breach site, arranging for medical attention for those injured by the mob or by the Crime Syndicate, and coordinating the National Guard response as the entire area was shut down and cordoned off. She was also taking rapid-fire notes on a tablet as she listened to someone on her headset.

"We're trying to get a head count of the speedsters," Iris told Barry as he and Cisco entered the room. "But it's not easy. You try counting a bunch of people who are scared and moving at seventy-five miles an hour."

"What's the estimate?" he asked her.

"At least ten thousand."

Barry whistled. Ten thousand speedsters. What were they going to do with them? He didn't think they could just send those people back to Earth 27. Not with Anti-Matter Man there. Even if they found a way to defeat Anti-Matter Man, Earth 27 would never be habitable again.

"We've got a problem," Oliver said, sidling up to Barry.

"It must be a day ending in Y," Cisco joked hollowly.

Oliver told them what he'd just learned from Felicity: Someone had used the Star City bombings as a diversion and broken into an A.R.G.U.S. lab. Something was stolen, but they didn't know what.

"Unless we're talking office supplies, I can't think of anything you'd steal from A.R.G.U.S. that would be safe," Cisco said with a shiver. "This is shaping up to be a crazy day, even for us."

Barry noticed that Oliver seemed antsy. Anti-Matter Man was a big problem, but someone on the loose with A.R.G.U.S. weaponry was a big problem, too. "Get back to Star City," he told Oliver. "Go track down this guy."

Green Arrow shook his head. "No. Nothing compares to the danger of that thing." He pointed to the big monitor, which showed the breach and—in the distance—Anti-Matter Man. "I'll stay here with you, but I need to send some of my people back to work the Ambush case."

"Hoss . . ." Wild Dog had been listening. "You know I'm no good with the universe-ending stuff. But tracking down some jerk who ripped off Dig's wife? I can handle that."

Oliver nodded. "Yeah. Take Dinah with you."

Barry had a thought. "Hey, Joe! What are you up to?"

Joe West looked up from the monitor Iris had assigned him to. "Just finished giving Singh a report. Why?"

"Want to go to Star City for a little bit? Help Oliver's crew out with some detective work?"

Joe considered, then nodded slowly. "Yeah. I can swing that with Singh. I'm due for shift change."

Barry turned to Oliver. "How's that?"

Oliver sighed and gave Barry a grateful look. "Perfect. Thanks." He jerked his head toward the big monitor. "Now let's figure out this guy."

• • •

Joe West didn't know from multiple universes. He didn't care about alternate timelines or parallel worlds. Super villains from another dimension were not his bailiwick. Going to Star City to catch a serial bomber and tech thief? Yeah, that was more his speed.

It's not that he wasn't smart. Joe knew that he packed considerable gray matter between his ears. Youngest cop to reach detective in the history of CCPD. Solved cases no one else had ever even come close to. He had the goods in the brains department. It's just that he cared most about the world beneath his feet, his family.

His kids.

Iris was the storyteller. From the time she could speak, she spun yarns all day long, jabbering and chattering whether Joe listened or not. Her dolls became characters in a sprawling, all-encompassing story line that Joe had privately thought of as the Dollpocalypse. "Daddy, this is Princess Garbie and she's Sleeping Beauty's best friend, but she doesn't sleep because she doesn't sleep and it's OK not to sleep and I don't like my bed so I'm sleeping in your room tonight and you go sleep on the sofa because that's where you sleep and you can take Princess Garbie if you want because she can keep you from being lonely."

She'd gone from inventing stories to figuring out stories as a journalist. Her detective skills rivaled his own, put to a different sort of service. Joe figured out stories all day long as a cop, assembling narratives presented piecemeal by the world, just as Iris did as a reporter. And now she applied her gifts to sussing out the story of solving problems at S.T.A.R. Labs. He couldn't be more proud.

And Wally . . . Joe had known Wally for only a couple of years now. Hadn't been there for the boy's childhood, a fact that snipped away pieces of his heart every time he encountered it afresh in his thoughts. But Wally had a head for mechanics, which, really, was just a variation on the same brainpower Iris and Joe evinced. Mechanics was the science of storytelling made solid. You swap plug and points instead of characters. You balance fuel mixtures and octane ratios instead of plot elements. But the goal was the same: Something that hummed. Something that moved. Something that *worked*.

And then there was Barry. Barry, Barry, Barry . . . The only one of his three children not of his flesh and blood, yet still bound inextricably to his heart.

Barry understood the alternate timelines, the parallel worlds, the universes beyond universes. Barry knew how it worked. He didn't need tools to see inside atoms—he could envision them in his head. Whenever Barry started to ramble on about brane theory and quantum weirdness (that was actually a scientific term!), Joe tended to tune him out, but he always did so with a smile on his face. It was good to see your kids loving something and excelling at it. He could still remember the first time Barry had come home from school with shining eyes and an A-plus on a science project. Unlike Iris, Barry was a quiet kid, but that day, he jabbered like an auctioneer hyped up on caffeine, his jaw going a mile a minute. Barry had found his love and his calling, and at the same time, Joe discovered something inside himself: a great swell of pride so powerful that it brought tears to his eyes and nearly knocked him off his feet.

On that day, in that moment, Joe knew for the first time that it didn't matter that Barry was the offspring of Henry and Nora Allen. On that day, in that moment, Joe knew that Barry was his son.

Joe thought all this in the time it took for Black Canary to engage the autopilot on the whacked-out sci-fi contraption she called the Arrowplane. And then there was a roar of engines, a lurch in his gut, and they were airborne—and Joe suddenly remembered that he really, really, *really* hated flying.

13

CISCO STOLE AWAY FOR A MOMENT to return to Madame Xanadu's bedside. He sucked in a breath as he stood beside her. She seemed to have sunk into a true sleep, though fitful, and he didn't want to touch her and risk waking her.

He didn't want to touch her, period. That last vibe had been painful and disorienting, and he couldn't be sure that he hadn't somehow harmed Madame Xanadu in the process. But he needed more information about Anti-Matter Man, and with her not-friend gone with the wind, he couldn't think of a better way to get it.

"Sorry if this hurts," he muttered, speaking both to her and to himself. He held a hand out, hovered it over her for a moment, then lowered it to touch the exposed flesh of her left arm.

And . . .

And . . .

And . . . ?

Nothing.

He frowned at his hands as though they were malfunctioning gadgets. He cracked his knuckles and tried again, this time touching her with both hands.

Still nothing.

Madame Xanadu snorted in her sleep, but otherwise . . . nothing.

Barry said she had magic powers. Not metahuman, but actual magic. What if she's blocking me somehow?

Another thought occurred to him. He reached into his pocket and withdrew the glowing green ring that Barry had taken from Power Ring. *Or what if it's this? What if this thing is stopping me somehow?*

The ring pulsated gently in his hand, but it was not the comforting gentleness of a parent's embrace or a friend's reassuring touch. It was the gentle pad of a lion on the veld, stalking its prey, the quiet, metered slither of a snake in the grass.

Cisco had faced Reverse-Flash and Zoom and Abra Kadabra. He knew evil when he saw it, but he'd never thought that evil could be in something inanimate, in something that wasn't alive.

Or is it? he wondered. *Is this thing alive?*

"Cisco, report to the Cortex, please."

He'd never been so glad before to hear Iris's voice over the internal PA system. He locked the ring in one of the facility's Danger Boxes, special lockers designed to contain the mysterious and just plain weird stuff they came across. Then he hustled up to the Cortex.

"Where's Dig?" he asked, looking around.

Iris was pacing before the monitor, running one hand through her hair while she twirled a pen with the other. She had voices bombarding her through her headset, over the speakerphone, and now from Cisco. She seemed uncharacteristically on edge. Then again, it was something like two in the morning by now, and she'd been working to coordinate emergency responses since sundown. She was entitled.

"Dig?" she asked, distracted. "He's with Barry at the breach site. They're gathering readings or something . . . No, no!" she shouted into the headset. "I need those ambulances at the stadium, not at the park! Divert them immediately!" She smiled apologetically at Cisco. "I need you to coordinate Barry and Diggle on this end. I can't break away from FEMA right now."

Cisco nodded and used one of the auxiliary control stations. He found Barry's signal with the S.T.A.R. Labs satellite and settled in.

• • •

Barry and Diggle set up the monitoring equipment no more than ten feet from the breach. The air blowing through had gone from fetid and hot to too cold. Anti-Matter Man was still quite a distance away, but now Barry had a better idea of his size. Like the stranger had said, he was at least one hundred meters tall, maybe more. And he was walking steadily toward the breach, in no hurry.

He's not even alive. Not even really a he. But all I feel coming through the breach is sheer malevolence. Sheer evil.

"It's like every bad nightmare I ever had has come to life and is making its way toward me," Diggle said with a deep and profound worry in his voice.

"That might be the most accurate thing anyone has ever said," Barry told him, and shivered. "Let's finish setting this up."

The monitoring equipment was mounted on a spring-loaded, gyroscopic tripod that had been designed to keep its balance no matter what. They used a series of threaded spikes to screw the tripod's feet into the ground. Dig grasped one of its legs and shook it, hard; the gyro worked—the monitoring lens didn't waver from its target, the breach.

"S.T.A.R. Labs, this is Flash. Are you reading the equipment?"

Cisco's voice came back. "We've got the money, honey. Come on home."

"You go through these things all the time, huh?" Dig said, gesturing to the breach.

Barry took in the breach once more. Everything through it seemed to have a dirty red film overlay, and there was a cloud of grit that swirled at the transition point. The edges of the breach were black and jagged.

"I don't go through *these*," Barry told him. "I've never seen one like this before. It's kinda—"

Just then, there was a rise in the wind, a howl like a lost wolf. Still far away through the breach, Anti-Matter Man raised his arm, pointing almost lazily at Earth 1.

Bolts of black lightning crackled, spitting through the breach, right at Barry and Diggle. Even for the Flash, there was no time to think. He just grabbed John by the shoulders and dragged him out of the way at superspeed.

The lightning followed.

Oh, boy, Barry thought.

Dig wasn't a small guy; he was big, with a big frame and lots of muscle packed on it. Muscle, Barry knew, weighed more than simple fat. What this all added up to was a heck of a lot of freight for Barry to be carting around. But he had no choice. He had to keep Dig out of the path of the lightning.

He couldn't just pick Diggle up and carry him—the guy was too heavy for that. But he could *push* him. So that's what he did—he got behind Diggle and pushed him along,

129

running at superspeed and using his momentum to keep Dig in motion, too. Zigzagging through the streets, the lightning bolt followed them, a dark and crackling harbinger of death.

S.T.A.R. Labs. There would be something there that could shield them.

The building was across the river. Barry took a short-cut, running himself and Diggle over the water so fast that they didn't have time to sink beneath the surface. *Surface tension—it's a Flash Fact!*

He couldn't see Dig's face, but he imagined it was etched with terror and shock. They'd only been on the move for about two seconds, but that was long enough for Diggle to register what was going on—lightning, danger, the world becoming a blur, his feet suddenly wet . . .

Barry pushed across the river and risked a glance over his shoulder. To his relief, the bolt of lightning shorted out somewhere in the middle of the river, sparking out of existence without so much as a pop.

He brought them to a gentle stop on the opposite bank, close to the back of the S.T.A.R. Labs building. As he caught his breath, he looked over at Diggle, who was whipping his head this way and that, disbelieving the sudden change in location. "What happened?"

"We outran a lightning bolt. Well, *I* outran it." Barry realized something. "Dude! You didn't throw up!"

Every time Barry had to move Diggle at superspeed, the man puked up his guts. But they'd just raced across half the city at the speed of sound and there was nary a splash of vomit to be found.

Diggle nodded, grinning broadly. "Check it out." He rolled up his sleeve to show off a flat square of material adhering to the inside of his left arm. "Military-grade anti-nausea patch. SEALs use them in rough weather. I figured I'd start wearing one and see if it kept me from hurling every time you decide to yank me across the country at Mach 7."

"Good for you!" Barry told him.

"My feet, though," Dig said with a strange expression on his face, "feel weird."

They both looked down. The soles of Dig's shoes had melted right off. His bare feet were sticking out.

"Not cool, Barry."

Things had calmed considerably when they got to the Cortex. Iris told them that she had sent Oliver to help keep the speedsters under control at the stadium. Right now, aid workers were distributing rations to a starving mass of speedsters who'd burned through their daily allotment of calories in mere minutes while running for their lives. Police and fire were where they needed to be and handling things on their own. Iris sank into a chair and seemed to melt.

"I'm exhausted," she said, "and I didn't actually *do* anything!"

"You did a lot," Barry told her, kissing her forehead. The night would become morning soon enough, and there would still be plenty for her to do. She didn't have a speedster's metabolism to keep her going. "Go get some sleep."

"Nope. Not until Oliver is back and tells me the Earth 27 refugees are OK for now."

"I'll wake you when he gets here. I promise."

Grudgingly, Iris heaved herself from the chair and went off in search of a bed. Caitlin finished applying a special salve to Diggle's speed-burned feet, then joined Barry at Cisco's control station, where he was bringing the monitoring equipment online.

"Give me some good news," Barry said. "We need to close this thing. And fast."

"Close it?" Caitlin asked. "What about the people over there on Earth 27? The ones who didn't come through? We can't just leave them there with that . . . thing." She flung a hand out at the monitor. Anti-Matter Man loomed large, no longer distant and distinct. He was much, much closer now, close enough that—without the blockage of people streaming through the breach—they could make out details.

He—it?—wore a reddish jumpsuit with a purple belt and boots. The sleeves were short and trimmed white, as was the collar. His skin was pale blue, except for the left side of his face, which was black. Perfectly round, perfectly blank eyes were set into a face shaped like an upside-down pear.

Beyond him: the rack and ruin of Earth 27.

Barry hesitated before he opened his mouth. Caitlin hadn't been there when the stranger with Madame Xanadu told them the sad truth about Earth 27—the planet was ruined. There was no home to return the speedsters to, and no way to survive there.

"Anti-Matter Man has already made it impossible to live there," he said gently, for Caitlin was a doctor—her entire life was about healing people and making it possible for people to live better lives. "His mere presence breaks down positive matter. The atmosphere over there is poison." He held out his hands, palms up, helpless. "There's nothing we can do."

Caitlin nodded, then shook her head, then nodded again, her expression troubled, her eyes clouded. "There has to be *something*," she insisted.

"They're all dead already," Barry said. "I don't . . . There's nothing. All we can do now is close that mega-breach so that Anti-Matter Man can't get through to Earth 1."

"Working on it . . ." Cisco said from his position at the

computer. He was fiercely mousing around, skimming the data streaming in from the monitors Barry and Diggle had set up at the breach site.

"Why don't we just use the quantum football?" Barry asked.

A couple of years ago, when he'd been relatively new at being the Flash, Barry had defeated the Reverse-Flash at the cost of Eddie Thawne's life . . . and at the cost of opening fifty-two breaches all over Central City. Metas came through the breaches, as did Zoom, an evil speedster from Earth 2. In order to close the breaches and force Zoom into a trap, Cisco had developed a gadget that could disrupt a breach's quantum entanglement with its home universe. They delivered this delicate, meticulously developed, crucial payload by, well, throwing it at the breaches.

It looked like a football. It worked on the quantum level. Barry called it the quantum football.

Cisco, of course, hated the name. "It's not a quantum football! It's a Portable Disentanglement Device. PDD."

"I don't care what it's called," Caitlin said quietly. "Will it work? Can we stop more people from dying?"

Cisco paused long enough to look over his shoulder at her. "I'll figure it out," he told her. "I promise."

14

FELICITY MET THEM IN THE BUNKER, a sheaf of papers in her hands. Without so much as a *hello* or any sort of preamble, she started handing out the papers to the three of them.

"Nice to see you, too, Felicity," Black Canary said.

"No time to greet." Felicity waved her own sheet. "Check it out: I cross-referenced high-tech thefts with Ambush's known demolitions over the past year. We know he swiped something from A.R.G.U.S. just now, but eight months ago there was an explosion in Hub City. That same night, there was a break-in at a decommissioned military facility just outside the city limits."

"No one made the connection," Joe said, skimming the paper. It listed details of the Hub City bombing and theft. "What does *matter transmission* mean?"

"Military jargon for *teleportation*," Felicity informed him. "Nothing was stolen from the facility, but it looks like someone may have copied data about a top secret Army research project on teleportation."

Wild Dog groaned. "More crazy powers. Every time you Flash people show up in town, things get weird."

"Be nice, Rene," Felicity admonished.

"Just show me something I can punch or shoot, Felicity."

Joe shook his head. "There's a time for that, but it's not now. We need more information. We'll start with the victim. We have to talk to this Lyla Michaels."

"Good luck with that," Black Canary said. "If she's holed up at A.R.G.U.S., there's no way to get to her."

Felicity grinned. "You'd think, right?"

Joe stood in a copse of trees in a small park right across the street from A.R.G.U.S. headquarters. There was a breeze coming down the main boulevard, and the trees shivered slightly. He turned up the collar of his coat. Colder here. And even though the sun should be coming up soon, it still somehow seemed darker than near sunrise in Central City. Star City in general just seemed a little grimmer, a little dirtier, a little more dangerous than Central City. Six hundred miles apart, but worlds away.

As he watched, a woman stepped out of the building, cast cautious glances in all directions, then wrapped her coat tightly around her body and jogged across the street. Lithe and clearly trained in fighting, she then walked with purpose, subtly checking her blind spots for tails or danger.

Joe sidled to his left so that he was more in shadow. As Lyla Michaels approached, he took his hands out of his pockets to show that he wasn't holding a weapon.

She darted into the copse of trees and looked around. When she caught sight of him, her expression of relief spent only a moment on her face before melting through surprise into tight, hardened outrage.

"Who are you?" she demanded, putting one hand in her pocket. "I was supposed to meet my husband here."

Joe held up both hands, palms out. "Ms. Michaels, please don't take out whatever crazy thing you have in your pocket. My name is Joe West. I'm a detective. You know my son Barry Allen."

Lyla's mien flickered for a moment, but she didn't move her pocketed hand.

"We had to spoof your husband's phone number for a text message. You weren't answering anyone else. And we're trying to help you."

"*We?*" she asked, eyes narrowing.

Aware that he was out in public and had to be careful with his words, Joe mimed shooting a bow and arrow, feeling like a complete idiot.

Lyla shook her head, her hand still in that pocket, clutching a heart-laser or a brain-zapper or a time-whatsis or whatever whacked-out tech A.R.G.U.S. had lying around. "This is an A.R.G.U.S. matter. We can handle it."

"Yeah, but are you handling it?" he challenged. "Look, Ms. Michaels . . . This is what I *do*. I'm a detective. You guys are great at mad science and keeping secrets, but I find things. I find people. Let me help you."

"We have a team that—"

"And they probably have to go through ten layers of government bureaucracy just to put their pants on in the morning, am I right?" He arched a knowing eyebrow, government employee to government employee.

Reluctantly, she chuckled. "And cops aren't hamstrung by bureaucracy?"

Joe shrugged. "I'm out of my jurisdiction. Not reporting to anyone. We both know that sometimes it's best to go around the usual procedures instead of straight through them. Am I right?"

She gazed at him unnervingly, not blinking, for what seemed a very, very long time. Joe began to wonder if time had frozen, and he was about to say something when she relented. "OK. I'll give you something to go on. Are you familiar with the Bug-Eyed Bandit?"

Stifling a groan, Joe nodded. Brie Larvan. Tech genius who'd invented artificial bees that did her bidding. She'd been fired from Mercury Labs back in Central City when her higher-ups discovered that she was weaponizing the bees instead of using them for peaceful purposes.

In her rage, she'd used the bees to kill two of her fellow scientists, Lindsay Kang and Bill Carlisle, and she'd been about to murder the head of Mercury Labs, Tina McGee, when the timely intervention of the Flash and the Atom saved the day.

Was there a lesson in all of it? He figured there was, and it was probably something like, "Don't tick off the woman who is weaponizing a swarm of robot bees."

"I thought she was in the hospital," Joe said. He'd heard that Larvan had ended up in Star City after escaping from jail but that her own bees had turned on her, stinging her into a coma.

"She is," Lyla said, nodding. "But we had possession of her swarm." She hesitated. "Keyword being *had*."

Joe nodded, catching on. "Got it. Thank you for your help. We're on it."

Lyla returned the nod curtly and turned to leave. Before she could walk away, though, Joe called out to her.

"I have to know—what do you have in your pocket?"

Lyla offered him a thin, brittle smile and withdrew her hand. In it, she held a partly used tube of lip balm.

Joe heaved out a breath. "I can't believe I fell for that."

"It's a very strong peppermint flavor, Detective. Don't discount its power."

15

BARRY ALLOWED CAITLIN TO give him a medical once-over, but then immediately dashed away from S.T.A.R. Labs, heading for the baseball stadium. It had been something like sixteen hours since he'd fought and defeated Rainbow Raider and the Seven Deadly Tints, but it felt like sixteen years. The world had been turned inside out since then.

Still, his exhaustion and the aches and pains stitched along his hamstrings, quadriceps, and trapezius faded as he stretched into the run. He took a leisurely pace to the stadium, arriving there after a five-second jog.

A series of fireworks exploded overhead just as he arrived. He ran up one of the ramps to the upper decks, emerging into the bowl of the stadium just in time to catch the last of the fireworks. Sure enough, Oliver was standing on the edge of one of the loge tiers, his bow in hand, having just launched a fireworks arrow into the sky.

Now that he had the attention of the stirring, chattering refugees below, he called out, his voice magnified by the stadium's public address system.

"I know you're all scared," he told them. "I know you're confused and worried. We're going to help you. You're safe now. The biggest threat to your safety is *you*. Please don't use your superspeed—you could hurt yourself or someone else. We have refugee services coming in to bring you food, water, and blankets. We'll be figuring out lodging logistics shortly. Thank you."

"Good job," Barry said, approaching from behind.

Oliver hopped down from the railing. "I sounded a lot more confident than I felt. Central City isn't set up for a refugee horde like this." He considered. "Back when it was Starling City, we had some experience dealing with massive numbers of displaced persons. After the Glades imploded. I'll have Felicity grab some of the relief plans and shoot them over to your mayor's office."

"Thanks, Oliver," Barry said, his voice suddenly clotted with gratitude. "I don't know where we're going to put all these people. Where they're going to live."

Oliver seemed puzzled. "Aren't we going to send them back to Earth 27? After we take down . . ." He hovered one flat hand as high up as he could reach to indicate the towering Anti-Matter Man.

With a tremulous sigh, Barry told him the harsh truth about Earth 27 and its environment. "So they're here to stay," he finished. "And we'll need to find a place for them."

Oliver grimaced. "Assuming *here* is still safe. Anti-Matter Man is getting closer to the breach, right? Once he comes through . . ."

"I don't want to think about it. We'll find a way to close the breach before then. In the meantime, I'm hoping there's a specific person among the refugees. I'm gonna go look."

"I'll get back to S.T.A.R. Labs and see if I can help."

Barry let him walk away, then called after him before he got too far. Something was nagging at him, and he had to get it out in the open. "Oliver, would you really risk maiming or killing one of the CSA? Just to get the others to cooperate?"

Green Arrow took a long moment, then threw back his cowl and turned off the gadget that distorted his voice. "That's the difference between you and me, Barry. I don't *want* to kill people. I don't *like* doing it. But if it's necessary, I'll do it. You . . ."

"I'll find another way," Barry said. "Because there's always another way."

Oliver shrugged. "If anyone else said that to me, I'd accuse them of sanctimony."

"But since it *is* me . . ." Barry said, drawing him out.

"We're built out of different parts, Barry. That's all. No good, no bad. No better, no worse. Just different."

Barry shook his head. "Same parts. Just put together in a different way. Our differences aren't as fundamental as you want to imagine."

Oliver gazed at him steadily for a long moment before speaking again. "At the end of the day, you have the luxury of being able to take all the time in the world to make split-second decisions. I don't."

It was true. And yet Barry couldn't help but feel that his way was the right way, the best way. Maybe it wasn't fair that he had an advantage . . . but unfair didn't have to mean objectively wrong.

He bade Oliver farewell, then zipped back down the ramps and out onto the field. To his surprise and pleasure, the Earth 27 denizens had taken Oliver's admonitions to heart. No one was using superspeed, and they all seemed to be settling down as Central City crisis workers wove through them, distributing aid packages of food, bottled water, and blankets.

He threaded his way through the crowd at a speed that usually made him invisible and utterly undetectable to mortal eyes. In this crowd, though, some of the Earth 27 refugees were attuned to the Speed Force just enough that they noticed *something* among them, twisting and craning their necks as he moved past them. It was an odd feeling, a sudden sense of vulnerability.

Near the third base line, he found the person he was looking for. Sitting on the ground, wrapped in a space blanket, the James Jesse of Earth 27 seemed shell-shocked and bereft. He was the leader of the Earth 27 Resistance, which had spent years fighting against the despotic, murderous reign of Johnny Quick. Once Barry had defeated Quick and imprisoned him, Central City was liberated, and James Jesse had taken on the task of rehabilitating the city and making it thrive again.

Now it was a dead wasteland, stripped of life.

"Hey. James." He vibrated back into the real world and put a gentle hand on James's shoulder. It was so odd—the Earth 1 James Jesse was a psychotic killer who called himself the Trickster. Seeing that same face pulled down into an expression of grief and horror shook Barry; his first inclination was to think it was a trap. But he reminded himself: *This is James Jesse, but it's not . . . James Jesse.*

James startled and looked up. "Flash? Is that you? But you went away. You . . ."

Barry crouched down. "Yeah, it's me. You made it to Earth 1."

With rapid blinks, James tried to process that. "I don't . . .

I don't understand. Earth 1? I just ran, like everyone else, from that . . . thing . . ." Shivers wracked his body and he pulled the space blanket tighter around himself.

When Barry had left Earth 27 the previous year, he hadn't had time to explain the concept of the Multiverse or parallel worlds. Now he gave James a quick primer, forcing himself not to delve into brane theory or quantum strings. *Just the facts and nothin' but,* as Joe liked to say.

"So we're on a world where there are others like us?" James asked. "Except they're all evil?"

Barry had never thought of it like that before. To him, Earth 27 was the "bad" alternate Earth, where the people he knew as good guys were bad. But to James, Earth 1 was the "bad" alternate Earth. He would get the shock of his life if he ever met the Trickster.

"The details aren't important," Barry said. "We need to act fast. I need to know a couple of things. The Crime Syndicate, to start."

"I saw them coming through. They broke Johnny Quick out of that prison you made for him. I'm so sorry."

"It's OK. I've already caught four of them, including Quick. They're locked up. All of them except for Owlman."

At the name, James's eyes bugged out. "Oh, no!" he whispered. "Not him! He's the worst of them all!"

Ultraman had all of Kara's powers and couldn't be

stopped by kryptonite. Johnny Quick was a superfast murder machine. Superwoman had a lasso that could choke you at a distance. Power Ring could conjure *anything* from thin air.

"The worst? What can he do? What are his powers?"

Ferociously shaking his head, James raised his voice. "No! You don't understand. He doesn't *have* any powers. That's what makes him so dangerous."

Barry cocked his head to one side. "I'm not following you."

James shed the space blanket and grabbed Barry by both shoulders, pulling him in close, their noses almost touching. His urgency radiated from him. "He's totally self-made. An inductive genius. Everything he is, he made himself. There's nothing to take away from him, don't you get it? He's the smartest man in my world, and he's spent his whole life training to be the best there is at *everything*. He's the most dangerous person alive."

Smartest man . . . "Is his name Clifford Devoe?"

James pushed Barry away and spat out a *Ha!* "Who knows? Who cares? He's insane and brilliant and you can't have him running around your world."

Great. Something else to add to the tote board. "We'll stop him," Barry promised. "One more thing: How did you guys create the breach to our world?"

Blank-eyed, James stared at him. "What do you mean?"

Barry ground his teeth. He was sympathetic to James's trauma, but he needed answers. "The breach. You opened it on your side when Anti-Matter Man came. To escape. We need to close it before Anti-Matter Man comes through."

James shook his head. "I don't know what you're talking about. We didn't open it. It just appeared in the city, and we ran through it. No one knows what it is. Or where it came from. We didn't open it, and we sure don't know how to close it."

16

EAR THE INTERSECTION OF
Kanigher Avenue and Heck Street, the breach
made a sound like a sigh, followed by a sound
like a transformer exploding.

Its edges rippled.

It *grew*.

And Anti-Matter Man drew closer.

17

JOE RETURNED TO THE BUNKER, where Wild Dog, Black Canary, and Felicity waited for him.

"Well?" Wild Dog asked in a tone of voice that said he didn't expect much.

"Bug-Eyed Bandit," Joe said.

Felicity dropped her teacup, shattering it on the floor. "Oh . . . great," she fumed.

First things first: Super-people had a nasty habit of defying the laws of nature on a whim. Just because Brie Larvan was in a coma in a Star City hospital didn't mean that she wasn't also somehow behind the explosions and the theft of her robot bees from A.R.G.U.S.

At the top of the agenda was Starling General Hospital, which still used the city's old name. They had to make sure the Bug-Eyed Bandit was actually, truly in a coma and incapable of masterminding this whole thing. Felicity was back in the Bunker, pulling data on the bees. Wild Dog had stayed behind in case an emergency came up and they needed him to roll on trouble.

Which left Joe with Black Canary. It was a little weird for him to sit in the car with Dinah Drake. He knew that she'd been a cop in Central City a while back. They hadn't known each other, but he'd seen her around the precinct.

Until the day he didn't. She disappeared. And no one talked about her. It was like she'd never existed.

Joe knew what that meant: undercover work. *Deep* undercover.

And then one day she was a Star City cop, just like that. Something had gone down. Something bad, he knew. It wasn't his place to ask about it, but the silence in the car was killing him.

"Robot bees," Joe muttered to break the quiet. "My life keeps getting scarier and more ridiculous."

Dinah smiled gently in understanding, but said nothing.

Joe waited a few more moments, then cleared his throat. "So, look, Barry asked me to tag along, but this is your turf. You take the lead; I'll hang back and back your play."

To his surprise, she demurred. "You have a ton more experience than I do," she said without a trace of ego or regret. "I'll follow your lead."

He opened his mouth to decline but realized that she wasn't just acting out of some kind of false humility or reverse psychology. She meant it. A good cop, then. A smart cop.

"It must have been bad," he said.

Her knuckles tightened on the steering wheel. Joe didn't know the city, so of course she was driving.

"Pretty bad," he went on. "Whatever it was that sent you out of Central, here to Star. It must have been pretty bad, is all I'm saying, and I'm sorry you went through whatever it was. The Job . . ."

She relaxed the slightest bit. "The Job is the Job," she said, finishing his sentence.

"Yeah."

They pulled up at the hospital just then. She parked the car at the curb, and they went inside, heading for the Coma Care Unit.

The unit was colder than the rest of the hospital. Was that some intentional effect of the heating-and-cooling system, or did it just *feel* colder because Joe knew who lay in beds behind all those doors flanking the corridor? The lights were dimmer here, too, and the whole place felt funereal.

A young doctor with bags under her bloodshot eyes

yawned and didn't even blink when they asked if Brie Larvan was still in her bed.

"Brie Larvan is *always* in her bed," the doctor told them, then led them to a smallish, darkened room. Lit by the phosphor of a brain monitor, Brie Larvan seemed horribly shrunken and withered. Joe knew she'd murdered two people and tried to kill many more, but he couldn't help experiencing a swell of pity. A life sentence in prison was one thing—a life sentence frozen in your own body was quite another.

"She gets moved twice a day," the doctor said with another yawn, "like all the patients. To prevent bedsores. But otherwise . . . This is it." She gestured down the length of Larvan's body. "What you see is what you get."

"And she hasn't left the room?"

The doctor opened her mouth to speak, then sighed and shook her head. Joe felt her resignation come off her in waves. If he weren't a cop, he was pretty sure she would have snarked something back at him.

Instead, she snatched up a clipboard from the bedside table and waved it at him. "Patient log. We notate every six hours. She's never left the room. Certainly not under her own power."

"Does she ever have any visitors?" Joe asked.

"Just one. He never stays very long. Just sits with her. I think he's family, but we've never really talked."

As Joe skimmed the clipboard, the doctor gestured to the monitor connected to Larvan. "The brain scan shows only limited activity. She can't generate the mental focus to sit up in bed, much less get up and walk away. Even if she *could* summon the willpower to do that—even if she woke up right now—her muscles have atrophied to the point that she'd collapse once she got out of bed." A pause. "Assuming she could get out of bed in the first place."

Touching Joe's hand to indicate that they should leave, Dinah said, "Thanks for your help, Doctor."

Joe grunted in agreement and handed the clipboard back. But just as he was about to cross the threshold into the hall with Dinah, he stopped and turned back. "Do you record the data from that thing?" He pointed to the monitor, which registered Brie Larvan's brain activity.

"Of course. It goes to a hard drive."

Joe whipped out his notebook and flipped through. "Can you check the following dates and times for me?"

The doctor's eyes widened for the first time, and she seemed to come awake. "Detective, I don't mind helping the police, but this is getting ghoulish."

Dinah agreed. "Joe, come on. It's a dead end."

Joe shook her off. "It'll just take a second. Four dates and times. Please, Doctor." He'd been a cop a long time. He knew when to get tough, when to bully and to bluster. He knew when to turn on the charm, to drop his voice an octave and purr like a kitten. But more importantly, he also knew when to beg. When to let his vulnerability and his need show through. Like now.

It usually worked on doctors. They wanted to help people.

"Doctor, please. We're in a tight spot and people could get hurt. We don't want to disturb your patient or cause her distress. I'm just asking you to look in your records and tell me if there was any unusual brain activity on these dates, at these times." He held out the notebook, where he'd transcribed from Felicity's notes the dates and times of the three bombings plus the one Barry had foiled, as well as their concomitant break-ins.

The doctor hesitated.

"Please," Joe said again, infusing the word with all the anxiety and thirst he could muster.

She drew in a deep breath, held it for a moment, then blew it out and took the notebook. "Give me five minutes."

Joe exchanged a triumphant look with Dinah as the doctor ambled over to the monitor and started tapping at a keyboard.

"Puppy dog eyes," Dinah whispered to him with a mix of admiration and curiosity. "Do they always work?"

Joe couldn't suppress the tiniest of deep-throated giggles. "Every time."

Soon enough, the doctor returned. She'd printed out a strip of paper from the machine, which she now marked up with a pen. "Here. I've marked your dates and times on here. There was no unusual brain activity, as you can see for yourself."

Joe and Dinah held out the paper between the two of them, their eyes scurrying back and forth along its path. There were occasional peaks and valleys in Brie Larvan's brain activity, but nothing exceptional, and nothing that coincided with the bombings and break-ins.

Their eyes met and they shared a mutual sigh of defeat. Joe was surprised how depressed he was to learn that Brie Larvan was *not* somehow telepathically controlling her bees and causing all this ruckus in the first place.

"Now if that's enough proof for you, Detective," the doctor said, "I *do* have other patients. They may be comatose, but they still need me."

Her tone was now brusque and wide-awake. Joe thanked her for her trouble and left her to her cold, dark ward with its cold, dark patients.

18

IRIS AWOKE WITH A START. SINCE THEY
spent so much time at S.T.A.R. Labs, they'd finally gone
ahead and converted some of the old storage rooms into
actual bedrooms. They weren't pretty—they tended toward
cinder block walls and bad lighting—but the beds were a lot
more comfortable than the ones in the medical bay.

She was alone. In the dark. Or so she thought.

Something . . .

Something was here. Some*one*—

Out of the darkness, a pale light flickered. And there was
Barry, standing before her.

He looked haggard, exhausted. His cowl was torn partly
away, and his costume was marred with scorch marks.

"Barry? What happened?"

He reached out to her. Something was wrong. Barry seemed . . . vague. Insubstantial. As though he wasn't really there. It wasn't the same effect as his vibration—it was almost like a bad TV reception, where there was so much static that you could barely see the image.

The tips of his fingers fell short of her by inches. She heard a low-pitched crackle around them as they jagged in and out of sight.

"I love you so much," he said, tears streaming down his face. "It'll all be OK. I promise. I will never stop loving you."

And then he was gone.

She was used to Barry disappearing in the blink of an eye, but this was somehow different. She had the sense that he hadn't run off, but rather that he had just . . . disappeared.

She sat up and flipped on the lights. Nothing. Nothing at all.

Iris shuddered and hugged herself tight. What was going on here?

A dream? A crazy nightmare?

She couldn't be sure. She *thought* she'd been awake, but maybe she'd been dreaming that she was awake. That happened sometimes.

That had to be it. She swung her legs out of bed and scrubbed her hands over her eyes. Too much going on. Not enough sleep. A world to save. It would mess with anyone.

Well, she was definitely awake now. Time to get back to work.

19

AMBUSH LICKED HIS LIPS AND guided the microforceps carefully. He had a magnifier hooked up to the desk now, its lens pointed right into the guts of one of the robotic bees. According to the schematics he'd been given, the bees could be reprogrammed by deactivating and then reactivating the miniature transmitter at their core three times in a row. It had to be done quickly, though, within a second or so: off, on, off, on, off, on. Rapid fire. Anything else would achieve nothing.

A bead of sweat formed on his forehead at his hairline and drizzled down his temple to his cheek, then traced a path along his jaw. He wanted to swipe at it, but he had just managed to pry apart some of the super-delicate fiber cabling in the main body cavity. Through the magnifier's lens, he could just barely make out a connection to what looked like the transmitter. At these sizes, it was tough to tell. He'd never met this "Brie Larvan," but she was clearly a technological genius.

And she must have had incredible patience and very steady hands.

The bead of sweat shivered and trembled on his chin. He ignored it and risked looking away from the magnifier for a moment, glancing up. He'd taped a large blowup of the schematic on the wall just in front of him.

Yeah. This was the transmitter.

The cable connected to the transmitter with the tiniest possible plastic clip, a little sliver of white. He'd been warned not to break the clip, which would permanently disable the transmitter and make rebooting impossible.

So . . . he had to disconnect and reconnect the cable rapidly, but also gently enough not to break it. And ideally without touching anything else inside the bee.

"How advantageous," he muttered to himself.

Fortunately, he would only have to do it once. Once one bee rebooted, it would send a signal to the rest of the swarm, rebooting the rest of them.

He managed to wedge the ultrathin end of the forceps under the plastic clip. He took a deep breath and then blew it out entirely, emptying his lungs. With a perfectly steady hand—the same kind of steadiness that rigged high explosives—he pried the clip loose. The cable came free.

OK. He had to move quickly. Closing the forceps to snag the clip, he guided it back into place. It clicked into position with a nigh-imperceptible jostle. Deep breath. Blow it out. He pried the clip loose again, then slid it back into place almost in the same motion. Perfect. Absolutely perfect.

One more time. One more breath. He slipped the clip out of its slot . . .

And the bead of sweat on his chin dropped, shaken off by his exhale.

It splashed onto the desk several inches from the bee, but its motion caught his attention, sudden movement out of the corner of his eye. Reflexively, he glanced in that direction, taking his eye off the bee's innards for a single, crucial instant.

The clip missed the slot. Hit something else. A contact formed between the cable and the transmitter, arcing through the metal of the forceps.

"Wait—" he said aloud, realizing he'd have to start over. But just then, he heard a sound.

A *buzzing* sound.

He jerked back from the desk, his vision swimming as it tried to adjust to the macro world, no longer focused through the magnifier. Blinking rapidly, he then rubbed at his eyes to clear them. The sound got louder and he spun around in his chair.

The swarm. Oh God, the swarm!

Behind him, the rest of the electronic bee swarm—which had been inert and deactivated—rose up from the carrying case he'd used to smuggle them out of the A.R.G.U.S. lab. His eyes widened in surprise and very real fear as he felt behind him for the special remote he'd stolen along with the bees. It was a master cutoff for just such an emergency.

He realized, to his horror, that he'd left the remote next to the carrying case. On the other side of the swarm.

"Whoops," he said.

And then the swarm attacked.

20

SO, WE'RE HOSED," CISCO SAID mordantly.

The sun had risen over the river, and everyone who'd stayed in Central City had gathered back at S.T.A.R. Labs: Barry and Oliver, Cisco and Caitlin, Mr. Terrific and Spartan. Iris stumbled into the Cortex, bearing H.R.'s favorite mug, which he'd left behind. It was a massive bowl with a handle, emblazoned with the legend TOO MUCH IS NEVER ENOUGH. She seemed put off and more tired, not less, for her nap, but her mien told everyone not to ask questions. Nightmares, Barry figured.

"Are we hosed again?" Iris asked, yawning. "Already?"

"I did all the math," Cisco said, "and there's no way to close the breach. The quantum foot—" He pulled at his ponytail. "Argh! The PDD won't be able to generate enough ionic energy to stimulate artificial quark sublimation because there's too much transuniversal interference at the intersectional vortices."

Iris mimed something flying over her head.

"I double-checked the math," Mr. Terrific offered. "It checks out."

"Thanks for the backstop, but no one asked you," Cisco said grumpily.

"Manners," Barry chided.

Cisco groaned. "Sorry. Bad mood. Bad day. If I didn't love my flowing ebony locks so much, I'd be tearing my hair out. I practically *invented* interuniversal transit, and I can't figure this out!"

Oliver stood under the big monitor, gazing up at the live feed of the breach, within which Anti-Matter Man grew larger and larger. "Not to reignite an old, sore topic, but . . . if we can't close this breach, we need to come up with a plan to deal with Anti-Matter Man. Preferably in a permanent way."

At the word *permanent*, Team Flash all glanced in Barry's direction. He gave it a moment's thought. "According to the stranger we met, Anti-Matter Man isn't really alive. I have no problem ending him," he said. "Anti-Matter Man isn't a person. He's a weapon that looks like one, is all. We should probably be calling him *it*."

Now they all stared up into the monitor. Anti-Matter Man had gotten even closer. That bizarre combination of colors on his outfit and on his skin might have made sense on Qward in the antiverse, but here it was almost clownish. He looked harmless and benign, and he was a destroyer of worlds.

"Cisco," Barry said into the pained silence, "I'm waiting for genius to strike."

"I got nothing." It obviously hurt tremendously for Cisco to admit it. "If I knew how the breach was opened, maybe I could reverse-engineer something. But the quantum noise is just too intense. Whoever established this breach did it in a hurry, without considering the way matter and energy flow between universes." He threw some numbers and graphs from his screen onto the big screen, overlaid on Anti-Matter Man. "There's interdimensional harmonics to consider. Transmaterial vibrations."

"It's like the difference between using a scalpel and a saw," Caitlin offered. "One gives you a nice clean cut, easier to control and suture. The other just rips through and makes it harder to put things back together."

Cisco snapped his fingers. "I got it!"

Everyone's excitement lasted precisely as long as it took for Cisco to point to Caitlin and shout, "Analogy Girl! *That's* your code name! No, wait—Dr. Simile! *Yes!*"

Oliver opened his mouth to speak, clearly annoyed, but Barry waved him silent. He knew how Cisco's mind worked, and he recognized some necessary blowing off of steam when he saw it.

"You said the word *harmonics* before," Caitlin put in. "Could we get Black Canary back here and use her Canary Cry? Stabilize the breach somehow?"

Mr. Terrific humphed and directed a T-sphere to the center of the room. "Checking your databases . . ." he said. "Pardon my hack."

The T-sphere grabbed the streaming data from the S.T.A.R. Labs computers and did some calculations. As they all watched, it projected a holographic chart into the air.

"I see . . . gobbledygook," said Caitlin.

"Fortunately, I speak fluent gobbledygook," Mr. Terrific said cheerfully. "Good idea, Dr. Snow, but it won't work. The harmonics of the breach are out of tune on both sides. You'd need to be on the Earth 27 side to make it work."

"And then you'd be dead," Oliver said with finality. "Look, we know who didn't open the breach—your friends on Earth 27. So . . ."

"If the good guys didn't open the breach," Iris jumped in, "maybe the bad guys did."

"So we have to go talk to the Crime Chumps of America again?" Cisco asked.

"Villains," Caitlin said. "So trustworthy. So willing to help."

The sarcasm was appreciated and also true. Still, they didn't have many choices. "Look, we need whatever help we can get," Barry said. "This is their world, too, now. If Anti-Matter Man gets here, they'll die just like everyone else. They're motivated."

"And they're super-evil," Caitlin argued. "How can you trust them? At their power levels, I'm not even sure how long the Pipeline will hold them."

"What about our own villains?" Iris said quietly.

Oliver folded his arms over his chest. "I hope you're not suggesting what I think you're suggesting."

"Let's hear her out," said Caitlin. "We need to close that breach, and we need to do it yesterday."

Cisco snapped his fingers. "Yesterday! Time travel!" He looked at Barry hopefully.

Barry shook his head. "Nope. Not into the past. I could make things worse. You know that. The last thing we need is to cause our own Flashpoint." At the confused looks from Team Arrow, he sighed. "I'll explain later. It's complicated."

Complicating it even further was an idea that had just popped into his head—the past was dangerous, but what about the future? Was there a way out of this crisis by going forward in time, not back?

He couldn't immediately think of one, but the idea nagged at the back of his mind. Probably because the stranger had mentioned the future and that had him thinking of Citizen Hefa and the sixty-fourth century. Just because he'd visited the future, though, didn't mean the world would necessarily be saved. The future was malleable. There were many possible futures, and Barry had seen two of them, both good.

They weren't guaranteed, though. He had to fight to make them happen. And that meant using every tool at his disposal. Even . . .

"Iris is right," he said. "We need all hands on deck for this crisis, and there are some very strong hands at Iron Heights."

"No!" Oliver slammed a fist on a desk. "Have you people lost your minds? We're already in the midst of a massive catastrophe, and you want to unleash super villains on the scene?"

"I'm getting desperate," Barry admitted. "So, yeah: If things get much worse, we might have to head to the metahuman wing at Iron Heights and see if we can get some help there."

"I'm with Robin Hood on this one. You're talking cray-cray!" Just to help Barry get the point, Cisco twirled his index finger around his temple in the universal sign for someone with a screw loose.

"When he's not in a power-dampening cell, Clifford Devoe is smarter than all of us put together," Barry argued.

"We're not busting the Thinker out of jail!" Cisco wailed. "It took us too long to put him there in the first place!"

"Got a better idea?" Barry shot back. "Because that guy"—he stabbed a finger at the main monitor—"is getting closer by the minute. Minutes are pretty long for me, but for you guys, time is running out. Fast."

Cisco shot a look at Mr. Terrific, who nodded grimly. "Give me and Mr. Wonderful over here half an hour. Seriously. Together, we're smarter than that jumped-up history teacher in Iron Heights. We'll figure this out."

Barry set his lips in a line, looking from Cisco to Mr. Terrific and back again.

"Give them a chance," Iris told him, touching his arm.

"Cisco's never let us down," Caitlin reminded him.

"And Curtis is the best," Black Canary said, to a firm, agreeing nod from Oliver.

Barry relented. "OK. Thirty minutes." He clicked a button, and a timer started on one of the auxiliary monitors. "To the very second. If half an hour from now, you don't have a solution, I'm taking my chances with the Thinker."

He took off, leaving a stunned gathering behind, their hair and clothes rippling in the wind of his departure.

Barry went to the Pipeline. He wasn't going to let the Crime

Syndicate loose, but Iris had made a good point about how if the good guys hadn't opened the breach, maybe the bad guys had. He could at least take another crack at getting the Crime Syndicate to open up. They were the most powerful people on Earth 27—they had to know *something*.

As soon as he entered the corridor in which the CSA sat in their cells, they all began hooting and hollering, pounding on the glass. Barry sighed and stood there, waiting patiently until—one by one—they tired and gave up. Ultraman, he noticed with some satisfaction, seemed to be the first to flag. With his incredible powers, he probably wasn't used to exerting himself, so he tired out quickly.

"Ready to talk?" Barry asked, gazing at each of them in turn.

Superwoman said something that Barry would never, ever repeat to anyone.

"Nice language," he told her. "Seriously, you guys are stuck here forever. Get used to those cages. Unless, of course, one of you wants to make a deal."

Crafty lights went on in everyone's eyes. Power Ring was the last to realize. Barry was now playing a game they were familiar with: The first one to talk got a deal. Everyone else would rot. It wasn't nice; it was pretty evil, in fact. Just the kind of thing to get the attention of a group of brutal thugs from the twisted world of Earth 27.

"What's the deal?" Ultraman asked.

"I'm not making a deal with this punk!" Johnny Quick shouted. It was still unnerving to hear Barry's friend Eddie Thawne's voice filled with so much rage and hate. "You can't trust him! If any of you tell him *anything*, I'll rip your hearts out at superspeed!"

"With what powers?" Superwoman snarked.

"Oh, I'll get my powers back," Quick swore. "I always do." He pressed up against the glass and glared at Barry. "Just you wait, you punk."

Barry sighed. "OK, so that's one out of four who wants to stay in prison forever. Anyone else?"

Power Ring crawled over to the front of his cell. His appearance was wan and sweaty. "Can I have my ring? Please? Just for five minutes. I swear I won't do anything bad with it. I just need to wear it. Please? I'll tell you anything you want to know. I promise."

Shuddering, Barry stepped away from the cell, even though Power Ring couldn't reach through it. He'd seen addicts in the worst of their throes before, and he recognized that look in Power Ring's eyes now. The ring he'd taken from Power Ring's unconscious body had filled him with dread when he'd touched it. Now that dread ramped up considerably. He was glad Cisco had locked it up tight. Anything so powerful that it could wreck a man so thoroughly was too dangerous to play around with.

Instead of answering Power Ring, Barry gestured to encompass all four cells. "Let's try this another way. I'll ask questions. You guys answer. Most helpful answer gets a reward. We'll figure out what kind of reward later."

Ultraman smirked and folded his arms over his chest. Superwoman grunted and leaned back against her cell wall. Johnny Quick sat down on his bunk and stared at the ceiling, pretending to ignore everyone. And Power Ring lay in a crumpled heap on the floor, mewling pitiably for his ring.

"How did you open the breach from your Earth to ours?" Barry asked.

For a moment, no one spoke, but then Ultraman barked a sinister yet genuinely amused laugh. "Craters of Wegthor! I'll answer that one. Because it won't help you at all. *We* didn't open it. Owlman did. And none of us know how."

"Traitor!" Johnny Quick howled, hurling himself at the glass with such ferocity that Barry had a moment of panic, thinking that the barrier would actually break. But it held, and Johnny collapsed to the floor, hissing in pain, his eyes locked on Barry, quivering with hate.

"Oh, shut up, you speedy little freak!" Ultraman snapped. "It's no good to them and gets me a reward. Right?"

Barry nodded absently. Owlman. The *fifth* member of the Crime Syndicate. He knew nothing of Owlman but what

James Jesse had told him. "He doesn't *have* any powers," James had said. "That's what makes him so dangerous."

He turned away from the villains, walking slowly down the hall. "Hey!" Ultraman shouted after him. "Don't forget my reward! You promised!"

Out in the corridor that led away from the Pipeline, he paused, thinking. Owlman had somehow opened the breach. But Owlman was missing. Had he even gotten through the breach? Was he still back on Earth 27, no doubt dead for his troubles? Or had he slipped through and—unlike the others—laid low, not drawn attention to himself . . .

Great. Do I have a genius-level super villain from another dimension loose in Central City? Again?

Iris popped around the corner. "You OK?" she asked.

"I'm all right. What about you? I thought you rested up, but you still seem exhausted."

"Flatterer," she joked, punching his shoulder lightly. "I just . . . didn't sleep well, is all. Too much on my mind, I guess. Weird dream."

"Wanna talk about it?"

She hesitated for just a moment, then shook her head. "No. Now's not the time. Bigger fish to fry, you know?"

He gave her a long hug. He liked to think that he had a pretty good string of smart decisions in his life, but marrying her had been the smartest. She gave him strength.

She made him a better hero and a better man. In her presence, exhaustion and pessimism could not abide. He wished he could flood her with the same relief she brought him.

After a few moments luxuriating in each other, she pulled away and jerked a thumb down the Pipeline toward the Syndicators' cells. "Were they any help?"

"A little. Maybe. Can you do me a favor?"

"Sure, what?"

"I didn't see a Big Belly Burger on Earth 27. Can you rustle up some burgers and sodas for them? Extra fries for Ultraman."

"Ultraman's lucky day," she quipped.

"Yep." He kissed her forehead. "Thanks. Talk soon."

At the stadium, he zipped around until he found James Jesse again. The Not-Trickster had his space blanket draped over his shoulders and was sipping hot soup from a steel mug.

"What more do you know about Owlman?" Barry asked without preamble.

James shook his head slowly. "I don't like all these Owlman questions. I hated Johnny Quick and the others, but Owlman actually scared the living hell out of me."

"I get that. So, tell me what you know so that I can make the problem go away."

"He was the crime boss of Gotham City, back on the East Coast. I never met him, obviously. Never interacted with him. He ran that place with an iron fist. I knew him by reputation, and that was enough."

Barry couldn't get over the idea of a super villain without powers, but then again . . . On Earth 1 there were plenty of heroes without powers. It made sense that there'd be powerless villains on Earth 27. "How did he keep up with the likes of Ultraman?"

"You don't get it. He was just human. And determined. And brilliant." Something occurred to James. "Why do you keep asking about Owlman?"

Barry hesitated. "No reason. Thanks for your help." He looked around at the milling masses. "We're going to figure out a place for you and your people, James. I promise. You won't be stuck here for long."

James offered his hand. "I believe you, Flash."

They shook on it, and Barry dashed back to S.T.A.R. Labs. Avoiding the Cortex for now, he ran to the subbasement, where he located the storage locker in which Cisco had secured Power Ring's gadget. His fingers hovered over the keypad. It was a ten-digit code to unlock the door, and then the glowing green ring and all its power would be at his fingertips.

Am I really this desperate? he thought. *Am I really going to try to wrangle something powerful and so evil?*

He punched in the first three numbers, then hesitated. His hand dropped to his side. No. It was too risky. He couldn't chance making the current bad situation even worse. He had to trust himself and his team.

Upstairs in the Cortex, Barry arrived in the middle of a raging argument between Mr. Terrific and Cisco. They were stalking around each other like rival lions, flinging their hands in the air, yelling.

Oliver stood off to one side, arms folded over his chest, mouth set in a grim, almost-out-of-patience line.

Caitlin lounged in a chair, picking at a paper envelope of Big Belly Burger Xtra Salty fries.

"What did I miss?" Barry asked.

"Thing One and Thing Two are unhappy with each other," Caitlin said, waving her fry-less hand in the direction of Cisco and Curtis. "Cisco says the flabbernasty won't jib-jab the grundlewhat properly, while Curtis believes Cisco's quantum whatchamajig will cause rampant mucus flooding." She grinned up at him. "Or something like that."

"Thanks for the update." Barry cupped his hands around his mouth and shouted, "Geniuses! Enough!"

Cisco and Mr. Terrific stopped arguing and looked over at Barry. Then they turned to each other and—inexplicably—bowed before backing away to separate workstations.

"They've been doing that the whole time," Caitlin

told him. "Curtis had this theory that if they let emotion override intellect, something might pop loose. So they've been screaming at each other in five-minute intervals, then bowing to show respect and no hard feelings."

"I really do love this guy," Cisco said, with a not entirely convincing smile.

"It's been half an hour," Barry said. "What do you have?"

Mr. Terrific and Cisco looked at each other, then at Barry, then at the floor.

"Nothing," Cisco admitted.

"The energy field is too intense," Mr. Terrific went on. "Planck's constant doesn't even hold at the very edge of the breach. Nothing we do will close the door."

"It's not a door," Cisco muttered somewhat irritably.

Barry groaned. He didn't want to carry through on his threat to release the Thinker from jail, but the image on the monitor showed the breach growing and Anti-Matter Man closing in. He had to hope that Clifford Devoe truly was the lesser of two evils in this—

"Door."

It was Oliver, speaking so quietly that Barry almost missed it.

"It's not a door," Cisco said again, this time definitely irritated. "It's a breach, a hole in reality. If it was a door, we could just slam it shut."

"You're being too literal, Cisco," Oliver said, striding quickly and with purpose so that he stood underneath the big monitor. He pointed up at the image of the breach. "Think metaphorically. You've been trying to close the door by pushing it. But what if you *pull* instead?"

Cisco shook his head. "You're not getting the science of this. There *is* no push. There *is* no pull."

"Oliver," Mr. Terrific said, "I mean no disrespect, but when it comes to this, you *are* a little out of your depth."

"I'm sure," Oliver said, smiling tightly. "But consider this: You've been trying to close it from this side. But it was opened on Earth 27. What if you tried to close it from *that* side?"

Cisco opened his mouth to shoot the idea down, but then stood there, frozen, his mouth open for several seconds.

"It's too toxic over there," Mr. Terrific said, glancing over at the stock-still Cisco. "Right, Cisco? Cisco?"

Recovering, Cisco said, very slowly, "That's . . . possible . . ."

Mr. Terrific blinked as Oliver's tight smile widened with satisfaction. "Well," Curtis said, "I mean, I *guess* . . . The quantum foam would have different characteristics over there. But it doesn't solve the problem of *how* . . ." He stopped and slapped his forehead. Then, in the same moment, he and Cisco said:

"A T-sphere!"

An instant later, they were at the clearboard, scribbling formulas and drawing schematics. Oliver sauntered over to Barry.

"Sometimes they just need a good, sharp jab in the ego," he commented.

"Good job, Oliver." Barry felt a tremendous sense of relief. The Thinker could stay in his cell at Iron Heights. The Crime Syndicate would remain in the Pipeline. And Power Ring's deadly, evil ring could remain unused and harmless in the safe deep in the S.T.A.R. Labs complex.

"As soon as they're ready," Barry said, "we can—"

"Ready!" Cisco and Mr. Terrific shouted out as one. They were standing at the clearboard, beaming. Curtis held aloft a single T-sphere.

Oliver smiled a genuine smile. "Even for Team Flash, that was fast!"

Barry and Oliver joined Cisco and Mr. Terrific at the breach site, just in case. The memory of the bolt of black lightning that had followed him and Diggle through the city was still fresh in Barry's mind.

Anti-Matter Man loomed impossibly huge and yet still impossibly distant.

"He doesn't seem to be in a hurry," Cisco mentioned, watching in awe. It was one thing to see the breach and the creature on the monitor. Quite another to witness them for real, up close.

"He doesn't have to be in a hurry," Oliver reminded them all. "He's a living engine of destruction. Now let's shut him down."

"On it," Mr. Terrific said. From a pocket, he produced the T-sphere he and Cisco had modified. "Off you go, little guy."

The T-sphere floated up from his outstretched hand and drifted into the air, picking up speed as it closed in on the breach. Barry noticed that both Cisco and Mr. Terrific had their fingers crossed as the little machine approached the tear in reality. Winds buffeted it, but it compensated, twisting and spinning in the air to maintain its course.

"Come on, come on . . ." Mr. Terrific whispered.

Yeah, Barry thought. *Come on.*

It hit the threshold between universes, jittered for an instant, then passed through. Cisco gave a little mew of satisfaction and triumph. Mr. Terrific whispered "*Yes!*" and fist-pumped. Barry relaxed.

Oliver . . . watched.

The T-sphere transitioned through the breach to the Earth 27 side. It spun in midair for a moment, as though orienting itself.

"It needs to detonate within three millimeters of the

breach edge on the Earth 27 side," Mr. Terrific told them all. "That will cause a quantum collapse that will basically mimic a local vacuum decay effect."

"It's gonna shut it down," Cisco translated for Barry and Oliver.

The T-sphere spun in a perfect circle, juked left toward the edge of the breach, then suddenly shot straight up in the air. They all craned their necks, tracking it as it reached the top of the breach . . .

. . . and then arced off into the far distance, disappearing from view before it could even reach Anti-Matter Man.

"What the heck, Mr. Not-So-Terrific!" Cisco exploded, rounding on Curtis. "What happened?"

"*You* tweaked the interdimensional-detection sensors!" Mr. Terrific complained.

As Curtis and Cisco argued, Barry and Oliver shook their heads at each other and took one step closer to the breach. The noisome breeze from Earth 27 had intensified. Anti-Matter Man was positively enormous at this point, still placidly walking toward the breach.

"This isn't good," Oliver said softly. "We're running out of options."

Barry gritted his teeth. Maybe it was time to consider . . . time. If he ran to the past, was there a way to stop all this from happening in the first place? The risk of causing something like Flashpoint was high, but at least the Multiverse would still exist, albeit warped . . .

No. No, he couldn't take that chance. The world was full of people making the wrong decision because they figured, "Well, it can't get any worse." But things could always get worse. He needed another way.

Was it possible . . . Could he run through the breach carrying some sort of weapon? Maybe get off a shot or two before succumbing to the poisonous environment?

Or maybe if he just carried a bomb and ran straight at Anti-Matter Man . . . A suicide run. But to save his world? Of course he would do it. In a heartbeat.

"OK, we figured out the problem," Cisco said, coming up behind them. As Barry and Oliver turned, he bowed and gestured to Mr. Terrific as though to say, *After you, my friend.*

"We got some telemetry back from the T-sphere before it disappeared out of range," Mr. Terrific said, consulting a glowing hologram projected by a second T-sphere. "It seems the transition zone between universes is screwing up the guidance systems on the T-spheres. It couldn't figure out where it was or where to go."

"Can you fix it?" Oliver demanded. "Right now?"

There was no hesitation in Mr. Terrific at all. "No. There are just too many variables to account for. Give me a day or two and yeah—"

"We don't have a day or two," Barry said. "We need to build a bomb and we need to do it now." He told them his plan, which—let's be honest—didn't take long. It was a pretty simple plan.

"No way," Cisco said immediately.

"Not a chance," said Oliver.

"I could totally build that bomb for you," Mr. Terrific offered enthusiastically. Then he noticed the expressions of shock and disbelief on Cisco's and Oliver's faces. "But, uh, I absolutely refuse to do so. You can't make me," he added for good measure.

"Guys," Barry said gently, "we don't have a choice. It's my life or the life of everything on Earth. Maybe everything in the universe, for all we know. This is easy math."

"There's gotta be another way," Cisco insisted. "We always find another way. That's what we do."

Oliver snapped his fingers. "There is!" He gave them all a moment to turn and look at him with incredulity. "I figured it out."

Cisco was the first to speak. "Look, uh, you're a treat with the bows and arrows, and I'm sure you're a smart guy in your own way, but . . ."

"But what Cisco is trying to say," Mr. Terrific said, leaping in diplomatically, "is that this is hard-core mad science here, Oliver. It's not really your bailiwick."

"They're right," Barry said with an apologetic tone. "Even I can barely keep up with some of the—"

"You're all idiots," Oliver said very matter-of-factly. "You keep thinking of fancy science, but what we need is something primitive." He turned back to the breach and mimed firing an arrow into it.

"Nice idea," said Cisco, "but there's nothing we can put on an arrow that would guarantee killing Anti-Matter Man. Plus, the windage and distortion effect of the transition between universes would be impossible to gauge."

Barry and Mr. Terrific nodded in agreement.

Oliver jabbed a finger in their direction. "First, never tell me what shot I can and can't make. Second, I'm not talking about hitting him. I'm talking about hitting the *breach*. You put whatever tech was in the T-sphere into an arrow. And then I fire it inside and hit the breach on the Earth 27 side to close it."

Cisco opened his mouth to shoot down the idea, but then a light came into his eyes.

"Is it . . . ?" Mr. Terrific said.

"We could . . ." Cisco said.

"No need for inertial . . ." said Mr. Terrific, and they started going back and forth, gesturing excitedly, not even finishing sentences:

"Reduce the profile by at least a centimeter . . ."

". . . no quark induction because . . ."

"If we adjust the eruption component . . ."

". . . nothing bigger than a teaspoon, right?"

They ran off together to the nearby S.T.A.R. Labs van and started rummaging through parts. Oliver allowed himself a small, satisfied smile.

Barry was a bit relieved but still uneasy. "Look, not to doubt you or anything, Oliver, but that's gonna be a crazy shot. You have to hit a target a millimeter wide, and you have to do it *after* the arrow goes through the transition zone. Are you sure you can do it?"

Green Arrow gazed into the breach, his jaw set, his eyes steely. "It's not about being sure. I *will* do it." Then he tilted his head to one side, as if thinking. "And I guess if I miss, we'll strap that bomb on you after all. That'll make you happy, right?"

21

JOE AND DINAH GRABBED A QUICK breakfast in a decent diner after their hospital visit. They agreed that Brie Larvan was legitimately not involved in the heist or the bombings. With nothing else to go on, they decided to check in with Felicity, but she called them just as they got back in the car.

Joe put her on speaker.

"Where are you guys?" Felicity asked them. "Wherever it is, change course. You're going to want to get to the 300 block of Grell Street."

Joe and Dinah nodded to each other. "What's on the 300 block of Grell Street?" Joe asked.

"Not what—who. Bertram Larvan. Brie Larvan's brother. Just found him in the databases."

"He must be the guy who visits her," Dinah said. "Do we think he's actually involved in the bombings?"

Joe shrugged. "Could be. But either way, he might have some sort of information that could set us in the right direction. There was this one guy I was looking for once in Central City. Ten years ago, maybe. My partner back then was Fred Chyre. We couldn't figure out where the guy was holed up. We went banging on every door, looking through every window in his neighborhood. Hassled his poor mother almost to death. She didn't know anything. Really, honestly didn't. But we just kept coming back to her. Knock knock on the door. All the time. Finally, one day, she mentions out of nowhere that her son used to collect baseball cards. Totally useless, right?"

"You found him at the *baseball card store*?" Dinah said with total disbelief.

"No!" Joe laughed. "But we did find a buddy of his there that we hadn't known about before. And that guy led us to an old girlfriend everyone thought had left town. And that led us to the guy. Good work, Felicity." He paused. "Felicity?"

"She hung up about halfway through your story about baseball cards," Dinah said, failing to hide a smirk.

Joe shoved his phone back in his pocket. "C'mon, let's go meet Bertram Larvan."

• • •

The building on Grell Street was nothing special, just a prewar brownstone with faded green shutters and a meager garden under the front window. Joe and Dinah climbed the steps to the front door. There was a set of three buzzers mounted next to the door, one of which was marked "B. Larvan."

Joe hit the buzzer. A moment later, a voice came through the speaker. "Yes?"

"Mr. Bertram Larvan?" Joe asked.

A small hesitation. Then: "Yes, I'm Bert Larvan. Who's this?"

"I'm Detective Joe West," Joe said, conveniently omitting exactly *where* he was a detective. He had no jurisdiction here, but there was no law saying that he couldn't talk to someone and ask questions. "I'm here with Lieutenant Dinah Drake. We were wondering if we could come up and talk to you? It's about your sister."

"Brie?" The tone of the voice changed, from bored and wary to concerned and interested. "Is there a change in her condition?"

There wasn't, of course, and Joe wasn't about to lie about that. But he had no problem letting Larvan *think* there was good news. "It's better if we come up and talk to you," he said.

A moment later, the door clicked open and a loud buzz filled the air. Dinah and Joe went inside, then up two flights of stairs to the third floor. The door to that apartment was already open, and a man stood there, waiting for them.

He had close-cropped black hair with a black soul patch and piercing blue eyes that drilled into them as they approached. "What's happened to Brie?" he demanded. "Tell me!"

"Could we come inside?" Dinah asked. "Sit down?"

He fidgeted but finally relented, stepping aside to usher them in.

The apartment was nearly bare. It was a studio with an archway into a kitchen area, but the rest of it was nearly empty. A futon was positioned against one wall, under a window, while a desk and computer occupied another wall. A stack of milk crates seemed to serve as a dresser of sorts, neatly folded and stacked clothes evident through the spaces in the walls of the crates.

"Nice place," Joe said, realizing even as he did how ridiculous it was to say. "I mean, uh . . ."

"High ceilings," Dinah supplied.

"Lots of natural light," Joe added.

Larvan crossed his arms over his chest. He had a way of holding himself such that his head was always tilted just enough to put his nostrils on full display. "I moved here from Opal City when Brie went into her coma. Haven't had time to buy furniture or anything. I spend all my time working or being with her. Now, what can I do for you?"

Joe glanced around the room quickly, taking it all in

with a detective's practiced eye. He'd developed something of a sixth sense for danger over his years as a cop. Nothing in Larvan's apartment was making it tingle. Yet. He spied a metal briefcase in the corner near a door that no doubt led to the bathroom. With his eyebrows, he indicated it to Dinah.

She understood instantly.

"Mr. Larvan," Joe said, taking out his notebook, drawing Larvan's attention away from Dinah, who was sidling over to the briefcase, "you moved here to help care for your sister?"

"What did I just say?" Larvan snorted. "Look, I have a lot to do. If you're not going to listen to me . . ."

"Sorry, just confirming." Joe pretended to make a note. He was actually studying Larvan. He'd come here thinking that he might learn something about Brie Larvan's past associates, but something in her brother's mien was ringing an alarm bell. True, most people were a little on edge around cops, but Bert Larvan seemed a little too annoyed. His body language—arms crossed, head cocked, jaw outthrust—was too defensive.

Something was wrong here.

"Did you know about your sister's criminal past?" Joe asked.

Another snort. "It was all over the news. *Bug-Eyed Bandit.* What kind of nonsense is that? Am I supposed to believe that it's not prejudicing the jury pool to impose an inane 'super-villain' name on my sister? My lawyers say that we have a strong appeal based on tainting the jury alone."

"Lawyers?" Joe actually made a note at this point. Behind Larvan, Dinah had sidled up to the briefcase. She edged farther out of Larvan's field of vision. "So you're trying to get her conviction overturned?"

"Of course! My sister never would have done any of the things she's been accused of."

"There were witnesses," Joe told him. Dinah flattened her back against the wall and *sloooowly* slid down to crouch next to the briefcase.

"Witnesses can be mistaken." Larvan was fuming, bordering on furious. "We're filing an appeal. And then we're going to sue Central City *and* Star City for everything they've got."

"None of that will help Brie," Joe said as gently as he could. "Money isn't going to wake her up from that coma."

"Well, maybe not, but . . ." Larvan suddenly turned around. "Hey!" he snapped at Dinah. "What are you doing?"

Dinah, hunkered down next to the briefcase, had just put a hand on one of the latches. "It's a nice one!" she said with false brightness. "I've been thinking of buying one of my own. How much did it cost?"

"Get away from it," Larvan ordered, his voice rising.

Joe and Dinah exchanged a quick glance, communicating volumes in that instant. Yeah, something was very, very wrong here. Larvan was far too protective of a simple briefcase. Joe was aware that this guy was suspected of involvement in a series of bombings, and he willed Dinah to step away from the case.

But she had different ideas. She hoisted the briefcase by its handle, standing as she did so.

"Nice and light!" she exclaimed, still pretending to be interested in buying one.

Gritting his teeth, Larvan snarled, "Put that down!"

"Hey, Dinah . . ." Joe said.

She ignored him. "It's like it's *too* light," she said. "Is there even anything in it?"

Larvan stomped toward her, but before he could snatch the briefcase, Dinah had already released the catches and the thing fell open.

And a swarm of bees poured out.

Joe shouted in alarm, but before he could do anything, the air around him went black with buzzing bodies.

22

CISCO AND MR. TERRIFIC COBBLED together something that looked very much like a wristwatch that had exploded in slow motion. Then they swiped Oliver's last remaining explosive arrow and disassembled it, putting their gadget into it.

They were long past Barry's original half-hour deadline. Anti-Matter Man was enormous, filling almost the entirety of the breach. He towered over everything in sight. Was he *growing*? The perspective was difficult through the distorting effects of the transition.

My God, Barry thought, staring at the way light warped where the universes intersected. *How in the world is Oliver going to make this shot?*

"OK," Cisco said, handing over the arrow. "Here's the

deal: You can pick your target. But it has to be where you see the ripple effect on the edge of the breach."

"And it has to be on the other side," Mr. Terrific reminded him. "So you'll need to—"

"Fire from the side at an angle," Oliver finished for him. "I have done this before, you know?"

"This?" Cisco asked, his voice squeaking as he flung his hands at the breach. "You've done *this* before? For real?"

Oliver said nothing. He moved several feet to the left so that he was seeing the breach at an angle of perhaps forty degrees. It was like shooting an arrow through an open door, trying to hit the very corner of the doorjamb on the other side.

Yeah, he told himself. *It's exactly like that. That's all it is. Shooting an arrow through a door. Right.*

"So, when it hits, one of two things will happen," Mr. Terrific said.

Barry arched an eyebrow. "Give us the bad news first."

"No bad news," Mr. Terrific said cheerfully. "Just two good scenarios."

"That's a switch," Oliver said under his breath, hefting the arrow, testing its weight and balance.

"In the first scenario, the breach folds in on itself, sealing off the portal between our universes, trapping Anti-Matter Man on the other side."

"And in the second scenario?" Barry asked.

"Well," Cisco said, "that one's a little less clear, but we think it's most likely that the breach seals on *this* side, but folds in on itself on the Earth 27 side, probably causing an explosion that would tear even Big Red there to shreds."

"So it's win-win," Mr. Terrific supplied.

"What if Oliver misses and hits the breach on our side?" Barry asked.

"I won't miss," Oliver said, not looking up for an instant from the arrow, which he was still scrutinizing.

Barry gave Cisco a *C'mon, level with me* look. "What happens if he misses?"

Both Cisco and Curtis seemed too intimidated to answer, but finally Cisco shrugged. "Nothing much. Probably some blowback energy from the impact, but the way it's rigged, it should just fizzle out on our side. And then Anti-Matter Man will come through the breach and kill us and every living thing on our planet, so we have that to look forward to."

"Which is nice," said Mr. Terrific.

Barry sighed. "Oliver, you ready?"

Oliver stared down at the arrow for the length of a heartbeat, then another. He knew that amount of time was an eternity to the Flash, but he did it anyway, because he needed to.

"Ready," he said.

• • •

Green Arrow paced backward ten yards from the breach, carefully monitoring and maintaining his angle. The wind around the breach was trickier than he wanted to admit. It was like firing an arrow into a hurricane and still needing to hit the target dead center.

Nocking the jerry-rigged arrow, he tried to clear his mind and found it was almost impossible. The stench. The wind. The knowledge that literally the entire world needed him to make this shot.

He inhaled and exhaled. All those years of training, the time on Lian Yu, in Russia, Hong Kong . . . The fights with Slade, the pain, the agony. All of it—all of his life, really—came down to this one moment. This one shot.

Gazing steadily down the shaft of the arrow, he could do nothing but stare into the breach. Anti-Matter Man loomed impossibly huge on the other side, so big and so close that he was visible only from his feet up to his chest. Any second now, he would crouch down, Oliver knew, and crawl through the breach. Or maybe he would just grasp its edges and tear it open wider, ripping the fabric of reality as easily as a child ripped paper.

"Here we go," Oliver whispered.

And he loosed the arrow.

For the first time in a long time, he fired an arrow and he wasn't 100 percent certain he would hit his target.

The arrow sailed easily in a fat arc on the Earth 1 side, then came down as it neared the breach.

Wind buffeted it. Oliver had deliberately aimed deep into the breach, knowing that the wind would push the arrow back toward Earth 1.

Sure enough, it wobbled in the air, struggling as it closed on the breach.

Had he chosen the right angle? Had he judged the wind properly?

The arrow sank too quickly, then picked up, tilting skyward as a gust caught it just right.

It went through the breach.

And just *barely* clipped the edge of the breach on the Earth 27 side.

Oliver's eyes widened and he was so ecstatic that he forgot to smile. "I did . . ." he started.

And—

23

—the world

went

white—

24

BARRY WATCHED THE ARROW catch on the edge of the breach as it passed through to the Earth 27 side. It was a perfect shot, one in a trillion, really. Oliver had done it exactly right.

His heart swelled and his face began to split into a huge grin when something happened.

Something unexpected.

He saw a wave of energy rippling out from the breach, carrying with it supercharged matter from nearby. It was like a massive tidal wave slamming into a beach, bearing with it all manner of flotsam and jetsam.

By reflex, Barry vibrated his body to intangibility in the nanosecond before the energy blast hit him. He threw up his hands to shield his eyes from the incredibly bright light, but even through his hands and closed eyelids, he could still see it, an impossibly white sheet of pure energy that, even in his intangible state, felt like a shower of hot needles.

It was gone in an instant. In less than an instant. It ended as soon as it began, in a time measurable only by someone with superspeed.

Barry relaxed his body's vibrations and breathed out a sigh of relief. Before him, the breach was gone. All he could see was the rest of Kanigher Avenue, two more blocks of damaged city street, and then a CCPD cordon down on Cary Street.

"Whew!" He chuckled, consoled by what he saw and by what he didn't see. "You did it, Green Arrow! You crazy Robin Hood!"

Turning to congratulate Oliver, he froze in place.

Oliver wasn't there.

Almost no time had passed at all. The arrow hit and then there was a nanosecond of energy. No time for Oliver to . . .

He spun around. Cisco and Curtis had been right behind him. They were gone, too.

All around him, he realized, the street was a wreck, even more so than after the battle with the Crime Syndicate. The S.T.A.R. Labs van was knocked to its side, its tires melted then resolidified, frozen drops of steel-lined rubber like black icicles.

The road looked like someone had pushed out a crater of black sand, then glued it in place. Nearby buildings were scarred and burnt into a dark rainbow of colors.

He swallowed hard, his stomach rising. Everything in him had gone suddenly, horribly, hollow.

I can't be the only one who survived. I can't be.

Barry looked for them. He looked all over. He scoured every last inch of Central City, vibrating through walls to foil locked doors, running up buildings to check in windows. Methodically and carefully, he searched everywhere.

It took ten minutes, that's how careful he was. Since becoming the Flash, he couldn't remember the last time he'd taken ten minutes to do *anything*.

They were nowhere to be found. And as best as he could tell, there was nothing alive in a two-hundred-meter radius of the breach site. Except for him.

A nanosecond. That's all it had taken.

"Oh no," he whispered, dropping to his knees. "Oh no . . ."

25

FELICITY WAS GETTING ANTSY. No pun intended.

She hadn't heard back from Joe and Dinah since they'd gotten to Bert Larvan's apartment. A part of her wanted to send Wild Dog over there to check up on them, but while Rene was a good friend and a reliable stalwart, he was also a shoot-first, say-*Oops*-later kind of guy. She didn't want to put bullet holes in Bert Larvan prematurely.

So she did what she always did when something was bugging her (no pun intended, again): She hacked.

She started with social media, which usually was a pretty good "in" to most people's lives. Bert Larvan, though, had no social media presence. That in and of itself was suspicious. No Twitter, no Facebook, no Insta. Nothing. She thought maybe he used an obscure alias online, so she checked Brie Larvan's social media, looking for a follower or a friend who might be her brother. Nothing there, either.

She cracked some databases and started running queries. A student-loan database coughed up his name—he'd borrowed money to attend Robinson University in Opal City. Good school. Excellent science programs.

With that information at hand, she jumped over to Robinson U and knocked on their door. Computationally speaking, of course. They had pretty good encryption on their main systems, but they had an alumni directory that wasn't quite as well protected, so she went in that way, running a quantum process to break the password.

While she waited, she had Rene go out and get breakfast burritos for them. As she was devouring hers, her system pinged her that it had broken in.

"Always when I'm eating," she sighed.

Rene shrugged diffidently and crammed more food into his mouth. No sympathy from that direction.

She coasted her wheeled chair over to the computer. She had hacked her way into Larvan's alumnus profile. It wasn't exactly a treasure trove of information, but there could be something valuable on the alumnus page. She spied his Opal City address, which she noted. That could be helpful—might lead them to some friends or neighbors.

She skimmed down the page. He'd listed a job at something called Opal City Pest Remediation, but he'd only been there a month. Hmm. Maybe someone remembered him, though.

She went down a bit farther.

"Oh no," she said.

Mouth full of cheese and bacon, Rene said, "What's wrong?" It came out *uts ong?*

"We have bug trouble!"

"You mean . . . big trouble?" Rene clarified, swallowing his food.

"No! *Bug* trouble! *Big* bug trouble! Larvan's an entomologist!"

Rene shrugged. "He knows words?"

"That's an *etymologist*! Very common mistake. An entomologist studies insects. Larvan majored in entomology in college."

Rene got it. "Are you saying . . ."

"I'm saying he's not just Brie Larvan's brother. He helped her design the bees! She's a mechanics genius— probably got the idea for robot bees by talking to her brother, the bug guy. They did it together!"

She spun around to her console and called Joe and Dinah.

• • •

Joe felt his phone buzz in his pocket, but right now there was another buzz he was more concerned about—the swarm of bees that seemed to be everywhere. He hadn't been stung yet, but it had only been a minute or so since the swarm vomited itself out of that briefcase. He'd never been particularly afraid of bees, but being enveloped by a whole swarm of them was a bit different from slapping one away at a picnic.

"I can't shoot a bunch of bees!" Joe yelled. Even if he could, a bullet could easily go through the swarm and hit Dinah or Larvan. "We gotta do something!"

He couldn't see her, but he could hear Dinah's reply over the loud buzz of the swarm. "Cover your ears!" she warned him. She didn't wait for him to comply. Drawing in a deep breath, she belted out a wave of sound that seemed too impossibly powerful to come from a human throat. Joe caught the beginning of it before he managed to clap his hands over his ears, but even that tiny taste made his eyes water and his teeth shake in their moorings.

Even with his hands over his ears, the sound was intense, piercing. He felt a filling in one of his molars loosen and tremble. Clenching his teeth to keep them in place, he squeezed his eyes shut, as though *that* would help.

Just when he couldn't take it anymore, it was over. He dropped his hands and opened his eyes.

Dinah stood in the middle of a bee apocalypse. There

were hundreds of the little critters scattered all over the floor of Larvan's apartment. Some of them still twitched legs or wings, but none of them were going to be flying anytime soon.

"What did you *do*?" Larvan wailed, flinging his arms out from his sides. "You destroyed them! How did you *do* that?"

The swarm had prevented Larvan from witnessing Dinah using the Canary Cry. For all he knew, she'd used an app.

"You're welcome," Dinah said with a huff.

"We all could have been stung to death," Joe said.

"Not me," Larvan retorted. "Brie programmed her bees never to harm either one of us. They recognize me by scent analysis. That so-called Mr. Terrific had to hack them to hurt poor Brie. Otherwise our safety is hard-coded."

"Well, that's nice for *you* . . ." Dinah said.

Joe checked his phone, which had stopped buzzing. Felicity had given up on a call and sent a text instead: LARVAN IS AN ENTOMOLOGIST! WORKED WITH B-EB!

Thanks, he texted back. *More soon.*

"You helped your sister build her bees, right?" Joe asked. "Or at least inspired the idea."

"Brie was—*is*—a genius," Larvan sniffed. "She didn't need my help."

Dinah shifted her stance a bit, keeping a wary eye on him. "But she knew about bees from you, right?"

Larvan shrugged. "She might have picked up a bit here and there from our conversations. It's not a crime to talk to my sister, you know."

Slipping his phone back into his pocket, Joe produced his handcuffs and rattled them meaningfully. "Bertram Larvan, you're in possession of stolen property—"

"Stolen?" Larvan clenched his fists and turned on Joe, his concern over the bees morphing into rage. "They're my property to begin with! I just took them back!"

"Yeah, well, you don't get to blow up a bunch of buildings and break into a government facility just because you think you were robbed," Dinah told him. She had a hand on her holster, just in case Larvan tried something else.

But Larvan seemed more perplexed than anything else, his anger mutating into bemusement as he looked from Joe to Dinah and back. "Blow up . . . Government . . . What are you . . . ?" His confusion blossomed into horror. "Oh my God . . . Those buildings . . . He *didn't*!"

Joe pursed his lips. "*Who* didn't? Your partner, Ambush?"

Larvan shook his head madly. "You don't understand. He's not my partner . . . He . . . He approached me a couple of months ago. Said he'd heard about Brie and he wanted to help. Said he could get ahold of some of her bees for me."

"You expect us to believe a Good Samaritan just dropped out of the sky for you?" Dinah said with some asperity.

"I swear it's the truth!" Larvan exclaimed. "All he wanted in return was some of the bees and some of Brie's old schematics. I said, Sure, why not? I figured maybe I could sell the bees to help pay for the lawsuit and get Brie into a private facility."

Joe had confronted and interrogated many a suspect in his career. He had a good built-in lie detector. He thought Larvan was telling the truth. Besides, he'd seen Brie in the Coma Care Unit; if she were *his* sister, Joe knew he'd do just about anything to get her out of there.

"What do you think?" Dinah asked him.

Joe shrugged. "You had no idea Ambush was going to blow up buildings to make this all happen?"

"No!" Larvan said. "I didn't ask for details. I . . ." He rubbed his eyes with both hands. "I just wanted a piece of Brie. I wanted her legacy. Her work. *Our* work."

Larvan seemed horrified and baffled all at once. He wasn't a master criminal, a Bug-Eyed Bandit. He was a somewhat jerky guy who loved his sister and was blind to her crimes. He'd been suckered into this.

Joe relented. He tucked the handcuffs away. There was still possession of stolen property to deal with, but they could handle that later. For now . . .

"Prove you weren't involved," Joe said. "Take us to Ambush."

Larvan gulped . . . but nodded.

26

ARRY RETURNED TO THE CORTEX. He stood in the doorway for a moment, unnoticed.

Caitlin, Iris, and Diggle were all huddled under the big monitor, which showed only the words *NO SIGNAL* in blue against a black backdrop. The monitoring equipment had been vaporized by the trans-dimensional burst of energy that had sealed the breach.

There was no easy way to break the news.

"Guys . . ." His voice cracked on the single syllable.

They all turned as one. "Did it work?" Iris asked, running to him. "Did it work?"

He caught her in his arms, folding himself around her.

Oh God, he still had her, and she still had him. But the others . . . Cisco's family. Curtis's friends.

Felicity. Oh, Felicity. And William, Oliver's son. An orphan now. Oliver left behind an orphan and a widow.

Barry squeezed his eyes shut against the tears, greedily inhaling the scent of Iris's hair. Shea butter and peppermint. He wanted to dissolve into her, to become nothing more than a thought in her mind.

A memory.

Like the others.

"Did it work?" Caitlin demanded. "You haven't answered."

"It worked," Barry whispered, and opened his eyes.

Diggle hooted and pumped his fists in the air. Caitlin applauded. Iris clutched him more tightly.

"Why are you so morose, man?" Diggle asked. "We won! Does S.T.A.R. Labs have a champagne budget?"

"We might have some old, fermented grape juice in Lab 12," Caitlin offered.

"Look," Barry said. "I don't know how to tell you this . . ."

And then, with Iris still clinging to him, he told them. His grip on her tightened as he did so, as though afraid that she would melt away with the news. Or, worse, pull away in outrage and disgust.

Caitlin's mouth hung open and she stood perfectly still, unable to move, unable to speak. Then, without a word, she turned and fled into the depths of the medical bay.

Dig's face went gray. He suddenly seemed a hundred years older. His eyelids fluttered and he felt around for something to lean on, finally finding a chair to slip into.

"No," he whispered. And then, louder, "God, no!" He buried his head in his hands.

"What . . . what are we going to do?" Iris asked, pulling back. Her eyes swam with tears and her lower lip trembled. "What do we do now?"

Barry shook his head. "I don't . . . I don't know." Names and faces spun in his mind. Dante, Cisco's brother. They'd been getting along well lately. How would he find the words to tell Dante that his brother was dead?

"It happened so fast," Barry said. "Even for me. I just . . ." He replayed it again in his mind. He'd been replaying it since it happened, wondering if he could have done something—anything—to rescue the others. But even for a superspeedster, when time is marked in nanoseconds, it's impossible to do everything.

"I'll call Felicity," he offered, feeling weak and lame. But it was the least he could do. Diggle seemed broken, the thinnest sliver of himself, slumped in the chair, staring off into a void only he could see. "I'll be the one to tell her."

"No," Diggle said, standing. He shook himself and seemed to regain a measure of strength and resolve. He laid a hand on Barry's shoulder. "It should come from me. I'll tell her in person, back in Star City. She'll need all of us around her."

"Dig . . ."

Diggle grimaced, his jaw set firmly as a bulwark against tears. "You know, once upon a time I was his bodyguard. It was my job to protect him. Why the hell didn't I do my job this time?"

"No one could have. He saved the whole world, Dig. Make sure she knows that. The whole world."

In a shaky voice, Dig said, "You and Oliver . . . You had your differences. But he always respected you, Barry. I want you to know that. He admired your optimism. And maybe . . . Maybe he was even a little jealous of it."

Barry was at a loss for words. "Thank you," he managed at last.

Dig nodded once, opened his mouth to speak . . . and then realized he had nothing to say. He left the Cortex.

Iris leaned against a bank of equipment. "We should find Caitlin. She and Cisco were close. I'm worried about her."

Caitlin chose that moment to emerge from the medical bay. Her eyes were hollow, haunted, and bloodshot.

"I don't even . . ." She gave up and gestured helplessly. "I don't even know what to *say.*"

Iris went to her and put her arms around her. "There's nothing to say. And that's OK."

Barry looked up at the monitor. NO SIGNAL.

Nothing to say.

27

BERT LARVAN LED THEM THROUGH grimy streets to a distinctly unsafe part of Star City. Ambush, apparently, was living in a hovel, a burnt-out, dilapidated building that was fit more for demolition than anything else.

How ironic, Joe thought. The man who bombed buildings hiding out in one that should have been bombed.

Don't do anything yet, Felicity texted. *I'm tracking you through Dinah's phone and I'm going to send Wild Dog as backup.*

Joe snorted. He'd been a cop for a thousand years. He had Dinah as backup, and she had superpowers as *her* backup. They would be fine.

"Nice neighborhood," Dinah commented, looking around. "What do you know about this guy?"

From the backseat, Larvan shrugged. "I offered to let him stay at my place. Or even put him up in a hotel. He said he'd rather stay here." He paused. "He had a very weird sense of humor."

"So, this guy has your sister's bugs . . ." Joe said.

"And maybe some kind of teleporter," Dinah reminded him.

Larvan's eyebrows shot up. "Teleporter? Are they real?"

"Who knows?" Dinah said diffidently.

"We're bringing you in," Joe said, "but only to get him to the door. Then you're back outside where it's safe."

Larvan made a show of glancing around the block. "Are you sure this is safe?"

"It's broad daylight," Dinah told him, then hauled herself out of the car. She yanked open his door. "You'll be fine."

Together, they went into the building. All of Joe's cop senses were on heightened alert. Something about dilapidated old buildings . . .

A smell enveloped him—rotten food and a very human sort of stink. He breathed through his mouth and looked over at Larvan, who had put a hand over his nose. Dinah coughed quietly into her fist.

Larvan pointed to the stairs. Joe went up, going as quietly as he could, but the stairs creaked no matter where or how he stepped on them. Halfway up the flight, he surrendered and jogged the rest, grateful that the whole staircase didn't just collapse under him as he went.

There were no lights. Actually, there *were* lights—mounted on the ceiling—but there was no power. The place was nearly pitch-black.

On the second floor, there were three doors, one of which was half rotted away. Larvan pointed to one of the other two. Without a word, Joe and Dinah took up positions, Joe to one side of the door, Dinah behind Larvan. They both had weapons drawn.

At Joe's nod, Larvan knocked timidly on the door. Joe frowned and mimed a stronger knock.

Larvan tried again. Nothing.

With a frustrated sigh, Joe reached over and gave the door a good, solid cop knock.

Still nothing.

He leaned over and put his ear to the door, listening for footsteps, for Ambush heading for a fire escape.

Instead, he detected a sound: a familiar buzzing.

Joe's eyebrows shot up. He tried the knob. It was locked, but the door was fragile, and he'd be damned if a cheap lock in a falling-down tenement would keep him from closing this case. Gesturing Larvan and Dinah to one side, he stepped back a few paces and kicked the door with all his might. It shivered in the frame but remained standing.

He gave Dinah a pleading look—her Canary Cry could take the door down, easy—but she shifted her eyes to Larvan and shook her head.

Right. Gotta maintain the "secret identity."

He kicked the door again. This time, it splintered at the lock and swung open. The buzzing sound grew louder. Joe drew his weapon and edged past the broken door, mindful of the now-sharp edge, and entered the apartment.

"Irwin Schwab?" he called out. "Ambush!"

"This is SCPD!" Dinah said, following him. "Stay where you are!"

The buzzing grew louder. They crept down the entry hall, past holes in the wall and peels of paint, into the open space of a ramshackle, run-down living room. It was nearly empty, except for a sleeping bag rolled up in one corner, a gas lantern, and then a desk against the wall, on which was mounted a complicated array of scientific equipment— magnifiers, lights, microscopes. They were plugged into a portable battery pack that rested on the floor. Taped to the wall over the desk was a sheet of paper: a schematic of a bee.

But that was all just detail. The real sight in the room was the human-like figure on the floor, writhing and moaning in pain, covered in a blanket of bees.

Joe froze for a moment, aghast at the tableau. He couldn't move. And then a sound startled him: Bert Larvan had followed them inside and pushed through them, running to the bees.

Joe almost grabbed him and yanked him back, but the swarm parted as Larvan neared Ambush. Right. Programmed not to hurt a Larvan. The bees dispersed; most of them ended up going out the window. Some of them drifted up into the corners where the walls met the ceiling.

The man they'd been swarming was in terrible shape. Every bit of exposed flesh on his hands, arms, feet, and face had been stung, repeatedly. He was a mass of welts, bruises, and hives.

"Good God," Dinah whispered.

Larvan was suddenly all business, rushing to Schwab's side. "He's in anaphylaxis!" he told them. "There's something in my briefcase that could help!"

Just then, Joe heard a rumbling outside. Peering out the window, he spied Wild Dog pulling up to the curb on his motorcycle.

"Wild Dog!" Joe yelled out the window. "Car! Briefcase!"

Wild Dog tossed off a quick salute. Moments later, they heard his feet pounding up the stairs. He dashed into the room bearing the briefcase, then came up short when he saw the man on the floor.

"Aw, heeeeeelllllll no!"

"Bees are gone," Dinah snapped, taking the briefcase.

"Bees did this?" Rene asked. "Man looks like he went through a meat grinder face-first."

Larvan unlatched the briefcase. "He's in severe trauma from the apitoxin, to say nothing of the pain from the stings themselves. Unlike biological bees, Brie's were designed with infinite sting capacity."

"Oh, good," Joe deadpanned.

"They were inspired by the paper wasp, the most painful of the beestings," Larvan went on, unfolding a square of green fabric he'd removed from the case. "The robots can sting over and over, as often as they need to, injecting toxin each time. When their supply of apitoxin runs out, they can still deploy their stingers to cause pain."

"Congratulations," Rene said, indicating the writhing man on the floor. "From the looks of it, they did just that."

"This can help," Larvan said, shaking out the fabric. "Something I helped Brie put together, just in case the bees ever got out of control."

It was a one-piece uniform of sorts, unadorned and baggy. It included a hood with a full-face mask that had large eyepieces and twin orange antennae protruding from the skull.

"A *costume*?" Rene said incredulously.

"A protective suit," Larvan snapped, "designed to shield the wearer from beestings and also to allow a measure of control over the bees through transmissions from the antennae. And as a bonus, it's lined with a gel-like substance that soothes and heals beestings. Help me get him into it."

Joe and Dinah helped out as Rene stood off to one side, shaking his head and muttering. Together, the three others got Schwab into the suit.

For several long moments, nothing happened. Except the man was no longer moaning and writhing in pain.

"Now what?" Dinah asked.

"Now we wait," Larvan told her.

At that instant, the man in the green suit sat bolt upright and peered around. They all jumped back at his sudden movement.

"Weight?" he asked with a voice a little too bouncy and mischievous for someone who'd almost been stung to death. "Hey, it's not polite to tell a guy he's put on a pound or twelve. Sure, I'm a little heavy right now, but who *doesn't* indulge during the big Arbor Day celebration?"

"What?" Joe blurted out.

"Oh, sorry, I misread. He said *wait*, not *weight*. Point still stands. Or does the stand still point? Hmm . . ." He stood up to strike a thoughtful pose and stroked his chin. "I always get confused by nouns that can be verbs, don't you?"

Joe nodded to Dinah. He drew his weapon and his handcuffs. She drew her weapon, too.

"Irwin Schwab," she said, "you're under arrest for—"

"Irwin?" he interrupted. "Irwin? The only people who call me Irwin are my mom and my dad and my best friend from kindergarten and all my elementary school teachers and the guys from the Army and the barista who makes my caffè mocha every morning and pretty much everyone else who knows me. I know I had a point in there somewhere."

Joe blinked rapidly. "*This* is a serial bomber and master thief?" A beat. "He sounds like Bugs Bunny on acid!"

"The apitoxin must have messed with his neurochemistry," Larvan said. "He's . . . loopy."

"No," Ambush said, sighing, "I'm *Irwin*. We just went through that. Hey, wait!" He stuck his index finger in the air. "I have an idea, even though a lightbulb has not conveniently appeared above my head! I'll be right back!"

Joe raised his gun. "You're not going any—"

There was a soft, hollow *POP* sound . . .

. . . and Ambush was *gone*.

"What's going on here?" Larvan howled in dismay and sheer bafflement.

"Teleporting . . ." Joe murmured.

"That's a thing?" Dinah asked. "For real?"

"I told you!" Rene exclaimed. "Every time the Flash people come to town, things get weird!"

• • •

Starling City Bakery hadn't bothered to change its name when the city switched from Starling to Star. The owner had declared, "We started as Starling and we're going to *stay* Starling, even when they decide to change the name of this town to just plain S City!"

The early shift was finishing decorating some meringue pies when a *POP* sound echoed in the confines of the kitchen. Everyone turned to see what it was—

—they caught a brief glimpse of a green figure—

—and then it was gone with another *POP*.

And so was a pie.

"Everyone just calm down," Joe ordered. The ramshackle apartment was a chaos of overlapping voices, rising in panic. Star City wasn't Central City—they weren't used to crazy stuff like teleportation here. "It's gonna be OK. I promise. I've seen this kind of power before."

"Take the creep who can teleport," Wild Dog said in a steady tone, "and go back to Central City with him!"

"I gotta say, Joe," Dinah said, "this is a little out of our wheelhouse."

"Will someone explain this to me?" Larvan demanded. "How can he just disappear like that?"

"There's no time," Joe said calmly. "But I've got this. Everything is under control."

Suddenly there was a *POP* right behind him. He spun around and raised his weapon, just in time to see the man in green appearing right before his eyes.

"Hey, Joe!" Schwab chanted. "Where you goin' with that gun in your hand?"

And then—*WHAPP!* Before Joe could move or even blink, something smashed into his face. Something warm and soft and gooey and . . .

Well, delicious, really.

"Did you just hit me in the face with a pie?" Joe demanded, clawing at the stuff on his face.

"Is it cliché or homage?" Schwab asked. "Who knows? The Shadow knows! Is that reference kosher? Who knows? The Shadow . . . Oh, I could do this all day!" He danced a little jig and jumped in the air, clicking his heels together.

Rene growled and leaped at him. "You ain't doing nothing all day!" he snarled.

"Double negative!" Schwab cried as Rene tackled him. "Double negative! Get a copy editor in here, stat!"

As Joe tried to clear the pie from his eyes, Dinah pushed a gawking Larvan out of the way, looking for a clear shot. But the way Rene was entangled with Schwab made it impossible.

"Little help here!" Wild Dog shouted. "He's slippery!"

"And you're adorable!" Schwab cried, then bussed Rene

loudly on the cheek. *POP!* He was suddenly up by the ceiling. Dinah shifted her aim there as he began to drop to the floor.

"Gravity! Right! I forgot!"

POP! And he was behind Dinah, taking her gun from her. She spun around just in time to see him *POP* away again, this time over by the window.

"He's got my gun!" she shouted.

"Who?" Schwab demanded, looking around. He saw it in his own hand and recoiled in horror. "Oh no! Don't shoot me! I'm young! I have so much to live for!"

POP!

The gun clattered to the ground, but Irwin Schwab was gone, and even though they waited for several minutes, this time he didn't come back.

Joe's phone buzzed. He used his forearm to wipe off the last of the meringue and answered.

"It's Felicity. Do we have a sitrep? I want to update the guys in Central City and get an update from them."

Joe looked around the room. Wild Dog was hunkered down, shaking his head in disbelief. Dinah picked up her weapon, looked out the window, and sighed in defeat. Bert Larvan stood in a corner, eyes wide, not moving.

"Sitrep?" Joe asked. "Uh, yeah. Situation . . . weird."

28

HOURS HAD PASSED. BARRY, Caitlin, and Iris were still in the Cortex. By now, they figured Dig had to be back in Star City, to break the horrible news to Felicity soon after.

As the day outside burned on, they'd all sunk into chairs. Barry had peeled back his cowl but otherwise hadn't moved in a long, long time. Eternities to a speedster.

Caitlin and Iris sat close to each other. Barry had rolled his chair a little ways off. Some part of him insisted that he didn't deserve the comfort of proximity to his friend or his wife. He'd been there, and he'd survived when Cisco, Curtis, and Oliver hadn't.

According to reports, CCPD still had the breach site cordoned off, even though there was no breach. It would take a long time to clear out the debris, assess the structural damage, and make repairs. Barry knew that he would have to get involved—as the Flash, he could speed up the process considerably—but right now he couldn't even convince himself to get up from his chair.

"Diggle must have gotten to Star City by now," Caitlin said out of nowhere.

"God, poor Felicity. I can't even imagine . . ." Iris gave Barry a significant look. One superhero widow was enough.

He would have to call Dante soon, he knew. He couldn't put it off any longer. It wasn't right or fair. But there was also a baseball stadium full of speedsters from another universe to deal with, and the crew in Star City probably needed help with the bomber . . . if they wanted anything to do with Team Flash at this point.

"I'll . . ." he started, and then broke off at the sound of footsteps in the outer corridor. Except for Madame Xanadu, still unconscious in her room, there was no one else in the building. Had the mysterious stranger returned?

Spinning around in his chair, he was shocked at the sight of the figure standing in the doorway. Iris gasped. Caitlin erupted in a squeaky sort of hiccup.

"Thanks for just leaving me to my own devices," Oliver Queen said. "You know how long it takes to *walk* here from downtown?"

Barry glanced over his shoulder at Iris and Caitlin. He witnessed two pairs of widened eyes and similarly dropped jaws.

"Oliver," he managed after a moment, rising from his chair on shaky legs, "is it really you?"

Oliver was taken aback. "Of course it's really me. The guy you abandoned."

"What do you mean?"

"What do *you* mean? I shot the arrow. Hit the target. There was a white flash of light, and when I looked around, there were Central City police surrounding the area and moving blockades into place. I must have blacked out for a second. Which is probably twice as long as it took you to get back here."

Barry approached Oliver, sizing him up, studying him. Every instinct in his body cried out that this was his friend. But how? He'd explored the breach site after the explosion of light. Unconscious or not, Oliver hadn't been there.

"What time do you think it is?" he asked suddenly.

Oliver frowned at him. "That's a ridiculous question." But he unsnapped a catch on his left gauntlet, revealing a digital panel there. "It's just after six in the morning."

Barry pointed to the clock on the wall. "No, Oliver, it's almost noon!" he said excitedly. "I thought the blast of energy killed you, but it didn't! It just pushed you forward in time!"

From behind him, the sound of two chairs rolling back and colliding as Iris and Caitlin leaped to their feet. "That means Cisco and Curtis . . ." Iris started.

". . . might still be alive, too!" Caitlin finished. She high-fived Iris and the two hugged. "They're alive!"

Oliver furrowed his brow. "What is going *on* here?" he demanded. "Wait . . . Did you all think I was *dead*?"

"Glad we were wrong," Barry said. "I'd hug you, but you're not that guy."

Caitlin wiped tears of joy from her eyes. "I knew Cisco couldn't be killed by something as simple as a Multiversal breach detonation."

"Curtis and Cisco are missing, too?" Oliver asked.

Caitlin bobbed her head. "But if you were shunted into the time stream, the same thing must have happened to them. They could pop up like you did, or maybe they're still stuck. But now that we know where to look . . ."

"We can find them," Iris finished, nodding triumphantly.

"Time to get to work," Caitlin said.

"I'll call Diggle before he gets to Felicity," Iris said.

"And I'll go find Cisco's quark-tracking equipment," Caitlin added. "He keeps moving it from lab to lab, but I'll find it."

As she and Iris rushed off to do their jobs, Barry offered Oliver a big grin and clapped him on both shoulders.

"If we're going to find those guys, we need to contact White Canary and the Atom and their crew on the *Waverider*," he said, his voice excited and alive. He raced over to the main computer bank and started typing. "Plus, we have to figure out what to do with the speedsters from Earth 27."

"And don't forget there's a mad bomber loose in my city," Oliver reminded him, coming over to watch him at the computer. "We need to get on that, too."

Barry nodded in agreement. "Yeah. Plus, if we're really going to earn our superhero credentials, we should try to figure out why Anti-Matter Man got cut loose from Qward. *And* track down Owlman, who started this whole mess."

Oliver blew out a long breath. "That's a lot on our plates."

Barry reached for the phone. "Yep. I guess I'm about to request some vacation time from Captain Singh . . ."

29

IDIOTS. FOOLS. MORONS.

Owlman knew one thing—

No, wait. Scratch that. Owlman knew *many* things. He knew, in fact, *all* of the things. All of the things worth knowing, in any event.

Coming through the breach into this alternate universe, he'd realized that the smart play—the only play, really—was to lie low and puzzle out the particulars of this world. The best way to conquer was to study first. Examine. Scrutinize. Then make plans. Then double-check the plans. Then triple-check the plans.

Then, and only then, did the smart man strike.

Smart, as opposed to the dunderheads in the Crime Syndicate, who had barreled through the breach and decided to start wreaking havoc right away. And as always, without him there to plan, they'd fallen out, bickering among themselves, doing more damage to one another than any enemy could ever hope to do. They'd divvied up America for just that reason—every time they were in a room together, they tried to kill each other. Only he, Owlman, had the brains to resist the temptation.

Among the other four, there weren't enough brains to fill a monkey's skull.

He, though, had thought ahead. He had come through the breach and immediately ripped off his mask. And his cape. In the chaos following the breach, he'd sneaked into a nearby clothing store and changed into a staid, boring business suit. No one would recognize him. No one would know.

And now, completely incognito, he was shuffling through a line of locals, who were queueing up just outside the cordoned-off area, receiving food and medical attention from some sort of benevolent local bureaucracy. He smiled to himself. These people were weak and soft. Soon enough, he would rule this pathetic world. Just as he'd ruled Gotham back on his own version of Earth.

Just then, a man in uniform snapped his fingers and pointed. Right at Owlman! "Hey!" the guy barked. "You!"

Outwardly calm and placid, he couldn't keep his heart from hammering. How could they know? How . . . ?

The cop came closer, head tilted, as though in recognition. But that was impossible!

"Hey," the cop said again, "aren't you Bruce Wayne?"

CHRONOCRAFT DESIGNATED WR-2055:
THE WAVERIDER
TIME/LOCATION: UNKNOWN

MICK RORY HEARD A NOISE LIKE an old man trying to clear his throat, then realized that its source was himself. He was groaning deep in his chest. Pain raced all over his body.

He was used to pain. Pain didn't bother him. But usually he knew where it came from.

The last thing he could remember was leaving the bridge with a sandwich. And then . . .

And then . . .

He sat up. He was at the center of a field of wreckage, still-hot plates of metal steaming and sizzling, bubbling fluids lying in puddles all around, shards of glass strewn about. Overhead, the sky was a sickly yellow, with ominous black clouds gathering.

There were three moons, one of them partly eclipsing another, the third a dull gray.

His legs wobbled, but he forced himself to stand anyway, leaning on one piece of metal that wasn't too hot. He recognized it, he realized. It was part of the hull plating for the *Waverider*.

He was in a field of wreckage from the ship.

And he was alone.

A buzzing sound emanated from somewhere nearby. Mick scrounged around and dug through the weirdly soft sand at the base of the piece of metal. After a moment, he unearthed a glowing sphere that flickered from white to yellow and back again. The buzzing—*bzzzzt! bzzzzt!*—stopped for a moment, and then a voice spoke.

"... chronal abnormality ..."

It was Gideon's voice. Mick was holding some component of the *Waverider*'s AI.

"... extreme danger!" Gideon went on amid the buzzing. "*Bzzzzt!* ... chronocraft, be on alert! *Bzzzzt! Bzzzzt!*"

"What do you mean?" he asked, shaking the stupid thing like a Magic 8 Ball. But Gideon couldn't hear him.

"... day Supergirl died," Gideon continued. "Be aware of ... *Bzzzzt!* ... on the day Su ... *Bzzzzt!*"

Mick dropped the Gideon component, letting it babble static to itself on the ground.

"Guys!" he shouted, cupping his hands around his mouth. "Guys!"

No one answered. He wished fervently for his flame gun; he was suddenly incredibly cold.

The black clouds advanced. Rain was coming.

Rain and, Mick was certain, something more.

TO BE CONTINUED . . .

Cisco and Curtis are lost in time! A lunatic is on the loose in Star City! Tens of thousands of superspeedsters need a home! And an evil version of Bruce Wayne is starting to make plans.

Sounds like our heroes have a lot on their hands, right? Well, it's about to get worse. The good news: They can look for help from Supergirl on Earth 38. The bad news: Anti-Matter Man has beaten them there . . .

ACKNOWLEDGMENTS

As usual, I have to begin with a shout-out to all Flash writers past and present . . . and this time to those who've made Green Arrow's bow sing! These folks hit the target every time, and I'm proud to slap their domino mask on my face.

I am grateful to the folks at Warner Bros. and the CW who made these books possible, especially Carl Ogawa, Amy Weingartner, Victoria Selover, and Josh Anderson, but also to Greg Berlanti, Todd Helbing, Sarah Schechter, Lindsay Kiesel, Janice Aquilar-Herrero, Catherine Shin, Thomas Zellers, and Kristin Chin.

And my undying thanks to my partner-in-crime and editor, Russ Busse, along with the rest of the hardworking crew at Abrams—including but not limited to Andrew Smith, Kara Sargent, Jody Mosley, Maggie Lehrman, Chad Beckerman, Evangelos Vasilakis, Marie Oishi, John Passineau, Alison Gervais, Melanie Chang, Maya Bradford, Kim Lauber, Trish McNamara O'Neil, Brooke Shearhouse, Borana Greku, and Liz Fithian.

My thanks once more to César Moreno, who brings the comic book heat with every cover.

Last but never least: My undying love to my wife and kids, who are so understanding when Daddy walks through the office door and vanishes into the Multiverse.

ABOUT THE AUTHOR

BARRY LYGA is the author of the *New York Times* bestselling I Hunt Killers series and many other critically acclaimed middle-grade and young adult novels. A self-proclaimed Flash fanatic, Barry lives and podcasts near New York City with his family. Find him online at barrylyga.com.

1

WITH THE WEATHER IN NATIONAL
City finally turning from a grim winter to a
pleasant and long-overdue spring, the tables
outside Noonan's were definitely in demand. But when Kara
Danvers arrived for brunch—late, of course—she was pleased to
see that her friends had already gotten a table. Good positioning,
too—far enough from the restaurant entrance that they wouldn't
be bothered by customers coming and going, but still far enough
from the street that the road noise wouldn't bother them, either.

"There she is!" James Olsen cried, and leaped to his feet,
applauding.

Before Kara could demur, the others followed suit—Lena
Luthor, Hank Henshaw, and of course her sister, Alex. They
all stood and clapped wildly. James even managed a piercing
whistle.

Kryptonians can blush just like anyone else, and Kara's
cheeks flamed red and hot with mingled embarrassment and

pride. All around her, patrons at other tables were joining in, even though they didn't really know why. There was just something infectious about applause, she supposed.

She essayed a brief little curtsy, which only spurred her friends on to even more applause.

"That's enough, you guys. Come on!" She waved them into silence and pulled over a chair. "Sheesh. Talk about embarrassing!"

"The youngest winner of the Wheeler-Nicholson Award in history!" Alex said. "That's something to cheer about."

"I was going to bring a big banner," James told her, gesturing as wide as his arms allowed. Given his height and arm span, that would make for a pretty darn huge banner. "About yea big. Lena voted it down."

"I knew you'd be thrown by even some clapping." Lena, Kara's best friend, leaned over and patted her hand. "I did my best to keep them all under control."

"Thanks. I appreciate it."

The Wheeler-Nicholson. After the Pulitzer, it was the most prestigious award in all of journalism, and now her name was added to the roster of those who'd achieved it. Maybe she *should* let her friends make a big deal. Just this once.

Kara looked around the table. Alex. James. Hank. (Or John. Or, more accurately, J'Onn, the Martian Manhunter.) Lena.

"Aren't we missing someone?" she asked.

Just then, a slender man with a thick mop of black hair sidled up to the table, hands clasped behind his back. Querl Dox, better known as Brainiac 5 or just Brainy, was a member of the Legion of Super-Heroes, a superpowered team from the thirty-first century. He had volunteered to spend some time in the primitive twenty-first century while Kara's friend Winn visited the future to help out the Legion. It was sort of like a temporal student exchange program, really.

"I apologize for my tardiness," he said. "I was unavoidably . . . delayed."

"He's addicted to Tetris," Alex said confidentially.

"You promised never to tell!" Brainy snapped. "My weakness is my own onus to bear, not a burden to be borne by those I call *friends*."

"It might be time for an intervention," said Hank.

"Says the man addicted to Chocos," Alex teased.

"I can quit anytime," Hank said. "I think."

"It's a fun game," Kara admitted. "There's no harm in getting caught up in it."

"I am on level seven thousand three hundred and twelve," Brainy confessed. "On that level, the . . . speed with which the pieces fall is quite exhilarating. And I find the music . . . jaunty."

"Oh, Brainy." Kara sighed. "You *do* have a problem, don't you?"

"Nothing that cannot be resolved with the application of huevos rancheros," Brainy said, sitting next to Kara. "Shall we order?"

James flagged down a waiter, and soon they were all ordering. Kara took another moment to look around the table as her friends laughed and chatted and caught up with one another. These moments—these messy, glorious moments of camaraderie—were what she lived for. No battle to wage. No super villains to thwart. Just sociability and friendship and love.

She'd lost a family when Krypton exploded. She'd found a new family on Earth when the Danverses adopted her. Then she'd rediscovered family on Argo, a surviving colony of Kryptonians that included her biological mother.

But this . . . This agglomeration around the table, this messy, chaotic, laughing, goofing collection that included the sister of a super villain, her cousin's best friend, a superhero from the future, a manhunter from Mars, and her own adoptive sister—this was the family she had built for herself. A family that had accreted around her. It was the family she was the most grateful for, one that came together through sheer force of will and mutual compassion. She loved them all so much.

"Look!" someone shouted at a nearby table.

"Up in the sky!" cried out someone else.

Kara did what everyone else did—she turned her attention skyward.

Unlike everyone else at the table, though, she could see quite a bit farther and much more clearly than mere mortals.

"Not a bird or a plane, I'd wager," J'Onn murmured.

With a combination of her telescopic vision and X-ray vision, Kara zoomed in on the thing overhead and tried to pierce the veil of smoke and flame surrounding it. It was roughly human-sized, she could tell, moving at an incredible speed in an arc over the city. Something—someone?—had hurled it with tremendous force across the sky, originating from who knew where. There was something in the composition of all that smoke that made it impossible for her to penetrate even with her X-ray vision, but she could tell that the thing's flight path was rapidly descending and that it would crash-land . . .

"In Governor's Park," she whispered.

At this time of day, with such gorgeous weather, the park would be teeming with families. It was one of National City's most popular spots on a beautiful day like today.

"I'm on it," J'Onn said with a brief glance at Kara. "Don't worry, anyone."

Kara clenched her fists. She was out in public. And even though Alex, James, and Brainy knew her true identity, Lena didn't, so she was stuck. J'Onn could run off because Lena knew he was the Martian Manhunter. But there was no ready excuse for Kara to—

James broke into her thoughts. "Kara, get to the CatCo offices and coordinate our team response to this!" He dropped a wink that Lena didn't see.

Kara breathed a sigh of relief and leaped up from her chair. "Will do, boss!" She favored him with a grateful smile and dashed away from the table with nary a farewell to any of the others.

An instant later, she ducked behind a stand of trees planted at the edge of the road to shield Noonan's from some of the street noise. No one could see her. At superspeed, she whipped off her Kara Danvers clothing, revealing the costume of Supergirl beneath. Half a second later, she was airborne, closing in on the hurtling object.

Supergirl, are you nearby?

The voice in her head was the Martian Manhunter. Telepathic communication always felt like remembering something mundane and long forgotten. She never got used to it.

I'm close by, J'Onn.

I'm going to start clearing the park, he told her. *But there are a lot of people. I need your help.*

Before she could respond, Kara "heard" a new voice intrude on the telepathic conversation. *Forgive me for hacking into your metaneural discussion,* said Brainiac 5, *but I wanted to tell you that Guardian and I are both en route to the park, as is Alex. And a DEO team has been scrambled, much like the eggs in my huevos rancheros.*

The DEO—the Department of Extra-Normal Operations—was a top secret government agency charged with protecting Earth from aliens and all sorts of superhuman threats. Alex was its director, and she was quite simply the best at her job. But at the end of the day, the DEO was still made up of human beings and they had the limitations of human beings. A team of agents wouldn't get to the park before the object crashed down, possibly killing hundreds of innocent people.

Supergirl considered for a split second. Her original plan had been to grab the object out of the sky. But it was moving with such incredible velocity that she couldn't be sure she would be able to stop it. There was a very good chance that its momentum would carry both it and her into the park, doubling the damage.

It was faster to take a straight shot to the park and help

J'Onn clear the area. She adjusted her flight path in midair and launched herself downward, fists out.

I've calculated the most likely collision point, Brainy told her and J'Onn, *based on current trajectory, prevailing wind patterns, and local gravity permutations. Impact is ninety-nine point two seven percent likely to occur within six meters of the carousel.*

The carousel. Great. If there was one place in the park guaranteed to be packed with kids and their parents at this time of day, it was the park's famous merry-go-round, which boasted three tiers of wooden horses, unicorns, winged frogs, and seahorses for kids to ride. In her mind's eye, Supergirl could see the moment of impact . . . the explosion of force as the carousel was smashed to pieces . . . bodies tossed into the air . . .

Nope. Not on my watch.

Well said! Brainy cheered.

Supergirl accelerated, then rapidly decelerated as the carousel hove into view. The Martian Manhunter was already there, snatching up a pair of kids and hustling them away. Supergirl landed just to the left of the merry-go-round and shouted, "Attention! Attention! We need to evacuate you! Now! Don't worry—everything will be all right!"

Then she moved at superspeed, grabbing up kids and their parents and shuttling them away to the edge of the park, where emergency services—alerted by the DEO, no doubt—were already stationed. She made ten trips in less than a minute, slowing down only to make certain she didn't hurt anyone while whisking them to safety. On her return to the carousel, she spied Brainy, Guardian, and Alex all hustling kids away from the impact zone.

Before she could say anything to her sister, her super-hearing picked up a whistling sound. She looked up again. The object had just breached the park's tree line and was now on its downward trajectory.

Ninety-nine point five nine percent chance now, Brainy told her.

"We don't need the updates!" she yelled, forgetting that she could speak to him with her mind. "Just keep moving people out of the way."

Brainy very calmly plucked a screaming toddler off the ground and levitated away, thanks to his Legion flight ring. *You don't have to scream,* he said. *I once evacuated the entire planet Mordan in time to save the inhabitants from the Fatal Five and a sun going nova.*

Sorry, she thought back to him. Then: *J'Onn? How are we doing?* She was keeping an eye on the object as it sped toward her.

All civilians evacuated within a one-hundred-meter radius. Get out of there, Supergirl!

She considered doing it. But who knew what would happen when this thing hit the ground? She wanted to be close by to contain an explosion or subdue a creature or whatever needed to be done.

Nah, she thought to him. *I'm going to stay and watch the fireworks.*

Supergirl! J'Onn screamed. Her head pulsed for a moment with something like a migraine. *Don't be stupid! Drop back!*

The object was practically on top of her now. It crackled and spat green-and-blue flames as it shrieked through the air at her. Her X-ray vision caught a break as some of the smoke parted and she thought she saw . . .

She dodged to one side as the thing hurtled past her. The air went hot and dry in its wake, choked with clouds of smoke, ash, and soot. With a thunderous roar, it hit the ground just in front of the carousel. The earth shook—she flashed back to the last moments of Krypton, as groundquakes wracked the planet, ferocious power trembling up from the radioactive, unstable core. Her parents put her in a rocket and launched her into space . . .

But this wasn't Krypton. It was Earth, and the planet wasn't exploding. Before her, the world had gone black and gray with smoke and dirt thrown into the air. She heard flames and the sizzle-crack of melting metal. There would be no rides on the carousel for quite a while.

Supergirl drew in a deep breath, then exhaled her super-breath, blowing a tunnel through the debris hanging in the air. A deep furrow had been carved into the ground in front of her, leading ahead toward what had once been the carousel. The metal framework looked like a birthday cake that had been left out in the sun too long, and the wooden animals were all singed and flickering with flames. She shuddered in horror but also in relief that they'd managed to evacuate the area.

Supergirl! J'Onn called. *Supergirl! Are you OK?*

Yep. She took a step forward and blew some more ash out of the way, then squinted at the clouds of particulate all around her. *Let's get a hazmat team in here. My microscopic vision isn't picking up anything alien or dangerous in the debris field, but we can't be too sure.*

I'll tell Alex. You're sure you're OK?

She grinned to herself. As Hank Henshaw, J'Onn affected the stern mien of a driving taskmaster, but the truth was that he saw in Supergirl and Alex reflections of his own departed Martian daughters. His fatherly affection was sweet, even when unnecessary.

Takes a lot to hurt me. Hang back and help emergency services. I'm going to check on this thing.

She walked along the gash the fallen object had cut into the ground. The furrow deepened as it progressed. A few feet from the carousel, it stopped, ending in a slightly wider crater.

Supergirl peered down there.

And gasped.

Lying in a four-foot-deep pit, smoke purling from his body, was none other than Superman.

And he wasn't moving.

2

BARRY ALLEN—THE FLASH—GRIMACED as he listened to the report from Star City. He stood in the center of the Cortex, the huge, circular chamber at the heart of S.T.A.R. Labs that served as a staging area for Team Flash. On the main monitor, Joe West was filling him in on the hunt for Ambush Bug. A hunt that was, by every metric that mattered, not going well.

". . . not that I'm making excuses or anything," Joe was saying, "but chasing a teleporter isn't easy."

"I've been there," Barry said, remembering chasing Shawna Baez, the teleporting metahuman criminal also known as Peekaboo. He'd finally captured her by shutting down the lights in a tunnel, rendering her unable to see where to teleport. That didn't seem to help in this case, though. Ambush Bug teleported willy-nilly, apparently not caring where he ended up. And there was no rhyme or reason to his "crimes," making it impossible to predict his next move.

"I wish we could spare some manpower to help you out—"

"Person-power," Iris interrupted him, clearing her throat significantly. Tapping away at a keyboard at a nearby workstation, she didn't even bother to look up.

Barry nodded. "Sorry, yes, of course. Person-power." Back to Joe: "But we have our hands full here, too."

Joe nodded, his expression weary but understanding. "We're doing the best we can. I just wish you hadn't taken Felicity away from us."

With Cisco and Curtis both lost in time somewhere, Barry had asked Felicity Smoak, Team Arrow's resident hacker genius, to join him in Central City and help out. Ambush Bug was a problem, yes, but recovering Cisco and Curtis, then tracking down Anti-Matter Man, ranked much higher on the priority scale.

Oliver Queen—Green Arrow—stepped into the Cortex. "Felicity's flight just landed. She should be here in a few minutes. How'd it go with the Legends?"

Barry shook his head. "No dice." He quickly explained his conversation with Director Sharpe. "We're on our own for this one."

Iris turned away from her keyboard for a moment, worrying at her bottom lip. "You know, Wally—"

"He wasn't on the *Waverider* when it disappeared," Barry assured her. "He was on leave somewhere in the late sixties. He's fine. And once we figure out how to get the others back, we'll get him, too."

"Unless he comes racing through that door on his own," said

Oliver, pointing to the archway that led out of the Cortex and into the rest of S.T.A.R. Labs. "That's possible, right?"

Barry shrugged a little more diffidently than he felt. "Theoretically, yeah. Wally could generate enough speed to propel himself through time and return to the present. But it's not easy."

Even as he said it, he thought about how easy time travel *could* be. There was the Time Courier, of course, but also the amazing Cosmic Treadmill, the device he'd used in the thirtieth century to run to the sixty-fourth century. Those millennia had sped by like leaves blown by a derecho. But Ava Sharpe had been right—even if he had a million time machines at his disposal, they'd be useless if he didn't know when in time to go.

"You know . . ." Oliver stroked his jawline, deep in contemplation. "This is just way too much of a coincidence. Anti-Matter Man attacks, the Crime Syndicate breaches to our world, and the Legends vanish, all around the same time? That's a little much, isn't it?"

Barry started to answer but was interrupted by a burst of laughter from Iris's workstation. She looked up guiltily. "Sorry, guys."

"What's so funny?"

Iris gestured vaguely in the direction of her screen. "I'm searching for anything that might give us a clue as to Owlman's whereabouts here on Earth 1. So, checking for anything out of sorts or out of the ordinary, I just stumbled upon this guy on Twitter who swears he saw Bruce Wayne right here in Central City."

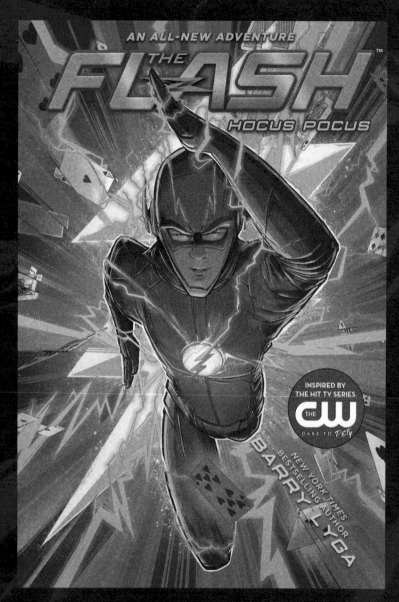